Of Night and Light

Stories

Michael C. Keith

BLUE MUSTANG
P R E S S

Blue Mustang Press
Boston, Massachusetts

© 2012 by Michael C. Keith.
All rights reserved. No part of this book may be reproduced in any form without written permission from the publishers, except by a reviewer who may quote brief passages in a review to be printed in a newspaper or magazine.

First printing

Cover Art: *Regatta* by Eric Michael Corrigan.

ISBN: 978-1-935199-15-1
PUBLISHED BY BLUE MUSTANG PRESS
www.bluemustangpress.com
Boston, Massachusetts

Printed in the United States of America

Author's Note

The stories in this volume first appeared in the following publications: *Eunoia Review, Bartleby Snopes, Greensilk Journal, Outward Ink, Static Movement, Blue Lake Review, Hogglepot Review, Connotation Press, Absent Willow Review, Diagonal Proof, Fictitious Magazine, The Sim Review, Danse Macabre, Orion Headless, Forge Journal, Fear of Monkeys, Quail Bell Magazine, Black Petals Magazine, Indigo Rising Magazine, Grey Sparrow Press, Subliminal Interiors, Ever After Review, Clever Magazine,* and *Lowestoft Chronicle.*

As with my two previous story collections (*And Through the Trembling Air* and *Hoag's Object*), I want to express my deepest gratitude to Susanne Riette, Christopher Sterling, and Nicki Sahlin for their generosity of time and precious suggestions. All the stories are better for their contributions.

A special note of appreciation is owed to Eric Michael Corrigan for the contribution of the book's cover art—*Regatta.*

The author would like to dedicate this book to his longtime cohorts, Alan, Terry, and Carl—dear and true friends through the *many* years.

Also by Michael C. Keith

Hoag's Object
And Through the Trembling Air
Life is Falling Sideways
Norman Corwin's 'One World Flight' (with Mary Ann Watson)
The Radio Station
Sounds of Change (with Christopher Sterling)
Radio Cultures
The Quieted Voice (with Robert Hilliard)
The Next Better Place
Dirty Discourse (with Robert Hilliard)
The Broadcast Century (with Robert Hilliard)
Queer Airwaves (with Phylis Johnson)
Talking Radio
Waves of Rancor (with Robert Hilliard)
Voices in the Purple Haze
The Hidden Screen (with Robert Hilliard)
Signals in the Air
Radio Programming
Global Broadcasting Systems (with Robert Hilliard)
Radio Production
Selling Radio Direct
Broadcast Voice Performance

Author's Note

The stories in this volume first appeared in the following publications: *Eunoia Review, Bartleby Snopes, Greensilk Journal, Outward Ink, Static Movement, Blue Lake Review, Hogglepot Review, Connotation Press, Absent Willow Review, Diagonal Proof, Fictitious Magazine, The Sim Review, Danse Macabre, Orion Headless, Forge Journal, Fear of Monkeys, Quail Bell Magazine, Black Petals Magazine, Indigo Rising Magazine, Grey Sparrow Press, Subliminal Interiors, Ever After Review, Clever Magazine,* and *Lowestoft Chronicle.*

As with my two previous story collections (*And Through the Trembling Air* and *Hoag's Object*), I want to express my deepest gratitude to Susanne Riette, Christopher Sterling, and Nicki Sahlin for their generosity of time and precious suggestions. All the stories are better for their contributions.

A special note of appreciation is owed to Eric Michael Corrigan for the contribution of the book's cover art—*Regatta.*

The author would like to dedicate this book to his longtime cohorts, Alan, Terry, and Carl—dear and true friends through the *many* years.

Also by Michael C. Keith

Hoag's Object
And Through the Trembling Air
Life is Falling Sideways
Norman Corwin's 'One World Flight' (with Mary Ann Watson)
The Radio Station
Sounds of Change (with Christopher Sterling)
Radio Cultures
The Quieted Voice (with Robert Hilliard)
The Next Better Place
Dirty Discourse (with Robert Hilliard)
The Broadcast Century (with Robert Hilliard)
Queer Airwaves (with Phylis Johnson)
Talking Radio
Waves of Rancor (with Robert Hilliard)
Voices in the Purple Haze
The Hidden Screen (with Robert Hilliard)
Signals in the Air
Radio Programming
Global Broadcasting Systems (with Robert Hilliard)
Radio Production
Selling Radio Direct
Broadcast Voice Performance

Contents

iDead	9
Late April Tree Frogs	19
Strategy	27
The Smell of Summer Asphalt	29
Little Conversations	35
People of Color	41
Incredulous	49
The Forcing House	51
Making Light	59
A Sticky Yellow Place	71
My Secret Tanzania	79
Gabriel's Response to a Casual Inquiry	89
Take the Second Left on Your Right	91
Road Kill	101
Redemption Lake	105
Baby Love	115
Fast Food	125
Things *Are* What They Seem	127
Barely	133
Light and Matter	143
Gloomy Girl	155
The Lonely Strand	157
The Chorophobe's Contrition	163
The Book Whisperer	167
In Response to the Brash Young Man	173
Dan the Man	175
In the Shadow of Light	183
Following Heather	187
Tele/kinetic	193
Years	203
On a Cold Damp April Night	209
Scar	211
A Better Life	217

Alme	227
Handy	233
How Chris Morgan Became a Street Person	235
Wanda Love Bobby	243
The Sweetening	247
Infantasy	253
Shedding Light	261
The Nature of Things	271
What He Remembered	281

*No matter how fast light travels
it finds the darkness has always got there first,
and is waiting for it*
—Terry Pratchett

iDead

Sometimes when you innovate, you make mistakes.
—Steve Jobs

A Pentagon black ops unit had worked on infrasound technology for years but never fully succeeded in demonstrating its efficacy as a weapon. When funding was withdrawn due to deep budget cuts stemming from a teetering economy, nominal monies were found at Hawley-Ailsworth Institute of Technology (HAIT) to continue development of a sonic and ultrasonic enemy deterrent.

For two years, graduate student Jesse Kline had worked as an assistant in HAIT's Infrasonic Emitter Laboratory (IEL). During this time he researched and wrote his dissertation on Otoacoustic Emissions, which he was slated to defend in ten days. It was his fervent hope that after his successful completion of his doctorate he would be hired fulltime by the Institute. He had worked hard to prove his worth to the project, and he had received glowing evaluations by its director, Dr. Phillip Leman.

No other student spent as much time at IEL as he had. In fact, it had become his second home. After working on complex tasks from Dr. Leman, he would often crash on a small cot in a storage room next to the lab. His dedication was both admired and mocked by his peers, who viewed him as a loner lacking in fundamental social skills.

"You redefine the term nerd, Jesse," commented a young colleague when his invitation to go for a beer was declined.

"Mark Zuckerberg and Bill Gates were nerds, too," responded Jesse, continuing to tap away at the keys of his computer.

Actual experimentation with the IEL sound emitter was off limits to student assistants without the presence of Dr. Leman, but Jesse had managed to assemble a crude, hand-held infrasound device on the sly. While he was uncertain just how powerful it was, he had a feeling its high-end beams were formidable, perhaps exceeding 10 megahertz. But there was no way of knowing what physical or neurological effects it might produce without an actual subject on which to test it. That was a problem until Jesse decided that he would serve as his own guinea pig. The design of his implement required a carrier, such as earphones, to detect its signal and relay it into the human auditory cavity. As irony would have it, Jesse discovered that an MP3 player could accomplish that purpose.

When the last of the student assistants left the lab for the night, Jesse set up his improvised instrument twenty feet from where he would direct its beam. After calibrating its target zone, he activated the wave emitter by setting its level at the low end of its spectrum gauge. He then placed the buds of a digital player in his ears and placed himself in the path of the beam. Within seconds he experienced slight nausea but nothing more until he increased the frequency output another increment. He then felt extreme dizziness and managed to remove the earplugs before toppling over.

He had succeeded in creating an instrument that would right an egregious wrong in his life—one that had resulted in the tragic loss of his father. Three years earlier, Liam Kline had been struck and killed by a driver using an iPod. Since then Jesse had put major effort into bringing about legislation that would end in-car use of the device. Despite his heavy workload, he devoted long hours with a local group to force his state to enforce the law against using any audio plug-in device while driving. However, thus far the state had remained unresponsive to their campaign, increasing Jesse's resentment toward those who behaved with callous disregard for others while behind the wheel. The state's failure to act had inspired Jesse's single-minded quest to create an acoustic bullet that would let him avenge the irresponsible conduct that had caused his father's untimely demise.

His plan involved zapping drivers that he could see were connected to audio players. He knew well the potential consequences of such an act, but he justified it on the grounds that it might keep innocent people from injury or worse. On the weekend before his dissertation defense, he removed his pocket size gadget from the lab after adding a finishing touch to it—a thumb size sticker from the CD of his favorite metal rock band. It featured a hideously carved jack-o-lantern with a pair of drumsticks tapping on its head.

"Perfect," he muttered as he climbed into his car to give his improvised emitter its first road test. It was not long before he saw a woman wearing an iPod bouncing to and fro behind the wheel of her car.

Let's see if we can make her refocus her energies, thought Jesse, pointing the sound wave gun at her and turning the dial to the second of five settings.

Within moments, the young lady became still. As Jesse let her move ahead of him, she pulled to the side of the road and leapt from her vehicle. As Jesse drove by, he saw her hunched over and vomiting profusely. A feeling of satisfaction overtook him and he set out to find another highway menace. By the time he reached home, he had caused the scene to repeat itself several more times.

* * *

Jesse spent part of the next morning reviewing his notes for his forthcoming defense at HAIT, and then made pancakes for his little sister and mother, a Saturday tradition.

"You're looking perky," observed his mother, as Jesse moved about the kitchen whistling.

"Never felt better," replied Jesse, flipping a pancake.

"Confident about Monday, huh?"

"That, too," answered Jesse, plopping a flapjack in front of his half-awake sister.

"Well, I'm glad you're in a positive mood. It's the best way to confront challenges," said Mrs. Kline, sitting next to her daughter.

"Piece of cake, Mom. Nobody knows more about Electrocochleography than your highly-gifted son," quipped Jesse, pouring syrup on his pancake.

"Well, don't get over confident, smarty-pants," remarked Mrs. Kline, smiling affectionately.

"Yeah, smarty-pants," repeated Jesse's nine-year old sister, Calen.

"No more pancakes for you, little sister," joked Jesse, moving to the stove, and placing a stack onto a dish. "Here you go, you guys. I have to get going. Work to do at the lab."

"On a Saturday?" asked his mother, helping herself to another pancake.

"The demands of genius never rest, dear family," replied Jesse, placing his dish in the sink.

"Will you be home for pizza night, genius?" inquired Mrs. Kline as her son took up his backpack and headed to the door.

"I'll return when great tasks are accomplished and extraordinary goals are achieved, mother dear. Later, you two!" replied Jesse histrionically.

Before climbing into his car, Jesse checked to make certain he had packed his wave emitter for the day ahead. He would park near the site of his father's death and wait in ambush for drivers lost in their downloaded tunes. In less than an hour he caused a half dozen drivers to lose the content of their stomachs. He then decided to take his reprisal to the next level by increasing his emitter's output. The elevated transmission resulted in the spinout of his first target. The Dodge Charger struck a utility pole, prompting Jesse to quickly leave the area. As he passed the crashed vehicle, he saw that its airbag had the driver pinned against the seat. The transgressor's arms were flailing about indicating that he was still very much alive. Rather than relief the motorist was alive, Jesse felt satisfaction over his victim's plight and vowed to continue his mission to punish motorists who disregarded the safety of others. It did not occur to him that his actions also endangered unsuspecting commuters.

* * *

Jesse spent most of Sunday in his room reviewing his notes for his final defense the next morning. He planned to continue his road crusade after first discussing his future prospects with Dr. Leman in the wake of his certain successful degree completion. With the freshly minted terminal degree in the bag, he would approach the lab director about a fulltime position at IEL.

That evening he took his sister and mother to miniature golf and after two rounds, which he won handily, treated them to ice cream sundaes.

"Sorry ladies," teased Jesse, "but it's simply impossible to repress my incalculable talent for all things competitive."

"Well, modesty is certainly not one of your gifts, Jesse," retorted Mrs. Kline, half-seriously.

"*Dr*. Kline to you," replied Jesse, stealing the maraschino cherry from the top of her sundae.

"Not yet, sonny. Not until tomorrow," and before her son could reply, she added, "I know, piece of cake, right?"

"Totally," answered Jesse.

Feeling thoroughly relaxed and confident, Jesse left for campus an hour before his meeting with his defense committee. On his way, he used his infrasonic emitter on two drivers, both of whom drove off the road after being zapped. This further buoyed his spirits and, by the time he reached HAIT, he felt invincible.

* * *

Jesse's major advisor, Dr. Carla Quinton, met Jesse at the door to the conference room and escorted him inside to his waiting committee. Surveying the group, Jesse felt renewed regret that Dr. Leman was not part of the proceedings. He declined to participate claiming that his close working relationship with Jesse created a conflict of interest. Despite Jesse's considerable efforts to persuade Leman, the professor remained adamant.

"You've been one of my student assistants for a long time, and if things work out, you may become a member of IEL's staff, so a little distance is prudent. We don't want to appear too cozy," contended Leman.

Although Jesse was disappointed by Leman's position on the matter, the director's words added to his hopes of future employment at the lab.

"Good morning, Mr. Kline," said Dr. Woodruff, chair of Jesse's thesis defense.

"Good morning, Dr. Woodruff," replied Jesse, taking the seat offered him.

Following an exchange of pleasantries, the inquisition began. For almost an hour, Jesse performed with aplomb, but then things took a negative turn as his outside reviewer, Dr. Everett from the physics department, took issue with one of Jesse's key contentions. Their debate continued for an hour with no resolution in sight.

"I'm afraid we appear to be deadlocked on this point. Sorry, Mr. Kline, but I don't see how we can sign-off on your dissertation until you make some significant revisions."

Despite Jesse's protests, the committee refused to approve his work until requested changes were made. Even his major advisor ultimately sided with her colleagues.

" Let's take this back to my office, before things get out of hand, Jesse," urged Dr. Quinton.

At that point, Jesse rose from his seat and stormed out of the meeting. When he was about to exit the building, he remembered the appointment he had made with Dr. Leman to discuss a position with the IEL. *Why bother after what just happened,* he thought, but then hoped Leman might be sympathetic to his predicament. After all, he had approved his original research proposal.

Jesse found the director on the phone when he reached the open door to his office. The professor waved him in, pointing to a chair.

"So, I just heard there were some bumps in your defense, Jesse," he said, placing the phone in its cradle.

"It's bullshit . . . I mean, wrong. Professor Everett has it in for me. I know that. He just refuses to accept a key point of my argument," complained Jesse, shaking his head in disgust.

"Dennis can be difficult, but I wouldn't get too upset. I'm certain you can make the changes that will bring him into the fold. He's not a totally unreasonable chap," offered Leman.

"On this, he's being completely unreasonable," replied Jesse, still fuming.

"I know why you're here, Jesse, but I think it might be better to have this conversation after you've settled the dissertation issue."

"So I have to compromise the integrity of my work to satisfy someone who's not even an expert in my field? Well, that's not my style. My research is solid, and he can go to hell," blurted Jesse, rising from his chair.

"That attitude isn't going to get you anywhere, Jesse. Calm down. You're going to ruin things for yourself."

"They're already ruined. This is a black mark on me at this place. I know that," growled Jesse, storming out of Leman's office.

* * *

On his way home, it occurred to him that he had seen Professor Everett listening to his iPod while crossing campus more than once, and a smile replaced his grimace. *He will get his*, thought Jesse, turning into his driveway.

As soon as he entered his house, his mother and sister greeted him with cheers.

"Hello, Dr. Kline," gushed his mother, and his little sister threw her arms around his waist.

"Leave me alone!" Jesse shouted, heaving his backpack onto the floor and dashing to his room.

"What's the matter, honey?" called his mother, as the room to her son's door slammed shut.

Jesse threw on his CD headphones, boosting its volume as he flopped on his bed. His dejected mother and sister could hear the strident licks of heavy metal guitars as they stood outside of his door.

"You'll get yours, Everett . . . you'll all get yours!" bellowed Jesse, hurling a pillow across the room.

"What's the matter with Jesse, mom?" asked Calen.

"I think I know," replied her mother gloomily, as she walked away.

Calen knocked on Jesse's door several times, but got no response. As she was about to join her mother, she noticed that some of the contents from her brother's discarded backpack had spilled out. Among the objects was Jesse's sonic wave shooter. It looked like a toy to Calen, who picked it up and, while playing with it, moved its dial to the maximum setting and pointed it up and down the hall.

After several attempts to communicate with her son, Mrs. Kline retired for the night. By late afternoon the next day, she decided to enter Jesse's room uninvited. It was something she never did, but his silence aroused her concern.

"Jesse?" she whispered, slowly opening the door. "Oh my God!" she cried upon noticing that the headboard of her son's bed and the wall behind it were covered with blood. Then her eyes came to rest on her son, who was missing the top of his head.

Late April Tree Frogs

Finally he paid the debt of nature.
—Robert Fabyan

Along the Calcasieu River north of Lake Charles, Louisiana, on high ground adjacent to a vast marsh, stood the 150 year-old former plantation that had housed the Arceneaux family for three generations. The ancestral moniker's reign would end with Claude Arceneaux, who had contracted a rare infection that left him infertile while serving with the army in the Philippines. He and his wife, Ruby, had broached the subject of adoption, but ultimately Ruby decided that if she couldn't bear her own child, she didn't want to raise somebody else's.

"Blood is what it's all about," she'd protest, as Claude tried to keep the subject alive.

"You'll be thinking otherwise when you're old and need someone to care for you," he would invariably reply.

"Hell, I'll hire someone to meet my needs with all the money you'll be leaving me. So hurry up and go," joked Ruby, and they would both chuckle, although feeling a tinge of emotional pain each time.

* * *

The Arceneauxs derived great pleasure in spending evenings on their expansive veranda when the weather permitted. It was something they did most nights. There they would talk, read, and even watch television. Claude had recently bought a small flat screen to use on the porch. His wife thought it was an unnecessary acquisition, since they already had a television that worked perfectly well. But Claude had finally worn her down.

"Okay, go get the silly thing," she conceded, throwing her hands skyward, and Claude wasted no time doing so.

"Can't beat a Sony. Look at that resolution. Don't get better than that," he said with boyish excitement while surfing through the countless cable channels.

"Our old outdoors set was just fine," responded Ruby, begrudgingly glancing at the television.

"Oh, c'mon, honey, you got to be blind not to see the difference," said Claude, with a slight edge to his voice.

"My eyes are perfectly fine, mister. They just don't see $400 worth of better there."

"Ball games are the best. You can see the faces of the folks in the stands," claimed Claude.

"You looking for somebody in particular?" replied Ruby, sarcastically.

"Could be. Maybe one of my old girl friends," responded Claude.

"Better check out the senior citizen seating then," said Ruby, suppressing a chuckle.

* * *

For the next several evenings, the Arceneauxs passed enjoyable hours in their outdoor sanctuary engaged in their individual activities—Claude viewing his favorite TV programs and Ruby lost in her latest romance novel. It had been the way they spent the warm season since they inherited the house from Claude's mother a dozen years earlier. The only thing that broke the silence was the singing of tree frogs, a sound they welcomed.

"Nature's serenade," commented Ruby, as she did every April.

"And they're in good voice, aren't they?" observed Claude, adding, "In fact they sound louder than usual. Don't you think?"

"Whatever," replied Ruby, immersed in her book. The following night, Claude again observed that the volume of the frogs was unusually high.

"Can't concentrate on the damn game with them croaking that loud," he complained to his unsympathetic wife.

"What's there to hear? Just a bunch of grown men chasing their balls, if you know what I mean," mused Ruby. However, the next evening, she admitted that the frogs' crooning was more boisterous than she could recall. "They must have added a bunch of new members to their choir," she quipped.

"Look there," said Claude, pointing to the edge of the porch where a half-dozen frogs had assembled.

"My lord, over there, too," commented Ruby, nodding in the direction of the porch swing.

"Jesus, critters are every where! Never seen that before," said Claude rising.

"Now don't you go squishing the poor things," warned Ruby.

"Think it's time for Corporal Arceneaux's 'Amazing Disappearing Froggy Trick,'" said Claude, stamping on the amphibian closest to him.

"Claude!!" shouted Ruby, horrified.

"Lookie here, my sweetie. Kermit done vanished into thin air. No sign of the little bastard," said Claude, raising his shoe to prove his claim. "Not even a water mark."

"That's disgusting!" bellowed Ruby, escaping to the house. In the Philippines, Claude had discovered that stamping on the small frogs that infested the jungle base caused them to evaporate. In one evening alone, for the fun of it, he had eliminated over two hundred frogs with the soles of his army boots. He repeated the feat many more times during his tour of duty.

* * *

The next night, while the croaking frogs sang even louder, they seemed to keep their distance from the Arceneauxs' porch.

"See, they know better than to come near Corporal Arceneaux," commented Claude.

"Yeah, they know you're a homicidal maniac," quipped Ruby.

It was not unusual for both Claude and Ruby to nod off in their wicker rockers as the evening passed. On one or two occasions, they awoke to find the sun rising over the mist-covered marsh. This time an odd noise stirred Claude. When his eyes gained focus, he saw that frogs covered his body as well as the entire veranda. He leapt to his feet shaking the frogs from his limbs. The noise that had broken his sleep occurred again and he turned in its direction. His wife was clutching her throat.

"Ruby, Ruby!!" screamed Claude, running to her side and whacking away the frogs that blanketed her pudgy frame. "What's the matter, honey?" It was immediately obvious to Claude that she was choking, and he lifted her out of her chair and began performing the Heimlich Maneuver. "My God, Ruby," he whimpered, as he desperately squeezed her limp body, but he could not dislodge what was clogging her windpipe. *She must have swallowed one of them damn frogs*, he thought, knowing how she slept with her mouth wide open.

When he failed to revive her, he called 911, but she was gone by the time the paramedics arrived. The coroner concluded that she had choked to death on a species of frog not known to inhabit the area.

"Not one of our local leapers. Not sure what kind it is, but I'm no newt expert. If I had to guess, I'd say it's one of them types come from the tropics. Maybe migrated up here," he told Claude. A week later the lab confirmed his suspicions.

"They say it's something called a *Lupon Striped Frog*. Mostly found in Southeast Asia. Like down in the Philippines. You were there, weren't you Claude?"

"Yeah, I was. Decades ago. But how could something like that get up here, doc?" asked Claude. "I mean that's on the other side of the world, for chrissakes."

"Can't say. Maybe someone let 'em loose in the marsh. You never know how things get where they get, but they do. Heard they found 'gators in Lake Michigan and a Polar bear was found walking the streets in Miami. Ain't uncommon for things to show up where they shouldn't," he answered.

* * *

In the weeks that followed, Claude grieved for his dead wife and wondered if his mass slaughter of frogs had caused him such misfortune. Since his wife's demise, he had stopped spending the evenings on his porch and had noticed that the amphibians' presence had dwindled as the heat of summer intensified. With their absence, he decided to return to the porch where he had spent so many wonderful evenings with his late spouse. While it didn't feel the same without her, something pleasant was resurrected when he returned to his old spot. It was in the late innings of a New Orleans Zephyrs game that he noticed several frogs had gathered next to the porch railing.

"What the . . .!" blurted Claude, jumping from his chair. "You goddamn things come back again? Well, I'll show you!" With great vengefulness he stamped on the frogs, which appeared to multiply with each vicious blow of his shoe. "I'll make every last one of you wart makers vanish! You took my Ruby, and this is what you get you when you mess with humans."

As Claude continued his assault on the creatures, he noticed that whole clusters of frogs seemed to fade away as he looked at them. It then occurred to him that they were shifting color to conceal themselves from the fury of his attack.

"You can't blend in, I know you're there," he spat, moving methodically along the full expanse of the deck to make sure he killed every slimy beast he could, even the ones he couldn't see.

Despite his thoroughness, the frogs continued to proliferate. Finally exhausted, Claude retreated inside only to encounter thousands of his adversaries clinging to the floors, walls, and ceilings. He waded though the swarming toads to the basement stairs and descended, returning moments later with a container of gasoline, which he quickly emptied and ignited. Using every bit of strength he could muster, he plowed through the quivering pile of frogs, escaping the house as it went up in flames.

"There!" he shouted at the top of his lungs. "Behold Corporal Arceneaux's 'Amazing Disappearing Froggy Trick!'"

* * *

The sky grew bright crimson as the flames shot upward and consumed the antebellum manse. Distant neighbors reported the blaze, but by the time help arrived, only a smoldering foundation remained of the once formidable dwelling.

"Too late," reported a firefighter back to his station headquarters. "The house is completely gone. Nothing left here at all. Might be bodies in the rubble. When the thing cools down some, we'll check."

What he failed to notice as he waited at the far edge of the lawn was a six-foot mound of camouflaged Luzon frogs that concealed the standing corpse of Claude Arceneaux.

Strategy

I am horrified of real thinkers.

When I come upon one,

my existence is voided.

Thus I travel with the inferior.

It is among them I thrive.

The Smell of Summer Asphalt

As rivers flow into the ocean but cannot make the vast ocean overflow,
so flow the streams of the sense-world into the sea of peace that is the sage.
—Bhagavad Gita 2:70

Rimyi Mehra could barely contain his excitement as the road repair truck approached his small village of Baritun. He loved the scent of fresh asphalt and the sight of the shimmering steam rising from it as it poured from the truck. But most of all, he loved to chew and blow bubbles with it before it hardened or was defiled by the wheels of ox carts, human feet, or the occasional automobile. No boy or girl in the village could create tar bubbles as large as Rimyi, whose favorite pastime was to launch his sticky black orbs onto the Yamuna River. He would follow them as far as he could and watch them bob and weave in the churning water.

The narrow main street of his village in the Haryana Region of India was repaved every year, due to the ever-crumbling ground beneath it. It was said that Baritun would soon slide from its mountainside perch into the Ganga tributary. But this had been predicted for so long that few people paid much attention. However, Rimyi was among those who did. With mounting fascination he measured the descent of the narrow strip of yard behind the two-room ghar he occupied with his mother and sisters. He had been born there eleven years earlier, the same year his father had left the family for work in Delhi and never returned.

As he and his friends happily followed the paver to the edge of Baritum, they heard screams. The weight of the truck was causing a section of the earth to move and slide into the river. Rimyi immediately feared for his family and ran home only to find it floating away. To his momentary relief, he found his sisters clinging to an uprooted Banyan tree.

"Rimyi! Rimyi!" cried Aaheli and Farha. "Yamuna has maatagee!"

After he helped his younger siblings from the fallen tree, Rimyi descended the landslide in pursuit of his mother, but the house had already floated far down the river.

"Maatagee! Maatagee!" shouted Rimyi, and his mother waved desperately from the roof of the dwelling that had been set violently adrift.

Although he was a strong swimmer, Rimyi knew he could not reach her without assistance. He scanned his surroundings for anything that would float but found nothing. An idea then came to him, and he scampered up the fallen cliff to what remained of the freshly paved road. Steam still rose from the asphalt, and Rimyi dug out a large chunk of it and returned to the river's edge. There he placed the tar in his mouth and rapidly chewed. Soon he was blowing the giant bubbles for which he was famous. In no time, he had a dozen or so, which he stuck together and placed in the stream. He then grabbed onto the flotilla and pushed it into the current with his sinewy legs.

* * *

Rimyi's makeshift craft gained speed as it moved past the verdant shores that led to the vast Guittar Pradesh Province. Only once had he been away

OF NIGHT AND LIGHT

from his native region when his family visited relatives in Ghaziabad. The large industrial city had both fascinated and repelled Rimyi. He found its ample buildings of cement, steel, and glass curious and longed for the modest, bougainvillea covered structures in his tiny village. The noise of the busy streets and the frenetic pace of Ghaziabad's inhabitants also offended his sensibilities.

"You are a true country boy," his mother had laughed, when he complained about the disagreeable urban surroundings.

Rimyi had not seen his floating house since he departed Baritun, and he was growing more fearful that it had sunk, taking his mother with it. Unlike him and his sisters, she could not swim, so the chance of her surviving in the roiling water without something keeping her afloat was unlikely. His anxiety mounted when the sun began to set over the rounded Vindhya Hills. He began to doubt if he would see her again, and he made a fervent plea to Vishnu to save her so they might be reunited.

"*Sri Govindaraja*, I serve you faithfully," he repeated, as he clung to his bubble raft.

When darkness overspread the land and water, Rimyi slipped in and out of sleep. He dreamed his sisters stood along the bank in flowing orange saffron robes and tossed magical *Rajanigandha* petals into the river for his safe journey. In his waking moments, he saw ancient temples awash in golden lights and he prayed each time for the restoration of his family.

As dawn drove the night from the East India sky, he passed the wondrous Taj Mahal, and its beauty lifted his mood and strengthened his resolve.

"I come for you, my maatagee . . . *I come!*" he shouted, the persistent current carrying him on his sacred quest.

In the light of day, Rimyi searched the river ahead for any sign of his mother but all that lay before him was endless miry liquid. He considered with dismay how his mother could have moved so far ahead of him, and he moved his tired legs harder to gain momentum.

As the morning deepened, his thoughts fixed on his sisters. He remembered them dancing gaily to their mother's sweet renditions of *Aloo Bolaa* ("Potato Says") and *Ek kawwa pyasathaa* ("There Was a Thirsty Cow"). *What would they do without her, and if he were to drown, what would they do without their big brother?*

"Lord Vishnu, I pray you give me strength," beseeched Rimyi, adding for good measure a denunciation of the forces of evil.

* * *

Young Rimyi pressed on despite the ache in his legs and his growing hunger. At what he calculated to be mid-afternoon, he spied a brilliant Royal Bengal Tiger drinking on the river's bank. Not much later, a herd of long-tusked elephants bathed as he drifted by them. He wondered if the sacred Yamuna purged animals of their sins as it did humans, and then he recalled a shaman explaining to the village children that animals were not capable of sinning. He wondered why people were.

Rimyi knew that the Yamuna flowed into the Ganga hundreds of kilometers south of his village. *Had his mother already reached it,* he pondered? Its waters were called *Amrita*—the nectar of immortality. Rimyi had learned this from his lessons in the Sanskrit, and it gave him hope that she had not perished.

The sun was hot against his skin prompting him to slip under his asphalt raft for momentary refuge. At night, the tar globes radiated warmth and protected him from the chilling effects of the wind. Time began to lose meaning to Rimyi as the sun and moon repeatedly appeared and vanished.

His strength waning, Rimyi now slept most of the time, the water lapping around his face. At one point, days into his seemingly endless journey, he saw–

–or believed he saw—a line of monks walking behind a funeral bier singing the *Bhajan*, his favorite devotional song and also that of his hero, Mahatma Gandhi. Fear suddenly seized him when the idea struck him that it might be his mother's body lying in repose atop the flower-covered catafalque.

"Maatagee!" he cried out, and the procession suddenly vanished before him as if it had been an illusion.

Other such visions came and went as he neared the confluence of the country's two great rivers at the holy city of Allahabad. He had never seen the Ganga and was excited, despite his intense fatigue. As the converged water widened, the balloons constituting Rimyi's vessel began to deflate one by one. He was soon treading water to remain afloat, but his spent legs quickly gave out and he sank below the surface. Blackness surrounded him as he descended the depths of the Ganga.

I am sorry, dear maatagee, that I have failed to save you and now I will die, thought Rimyi, as he felt his lungs contract and his life seep away.

* * *

"Rimyi, Rimyi," called a familiar voice from the void, and then the darkness lifted, and he beheld his mother sitting lotus-style under a fig-laden Bodhi Tree. "We are reborn in the subterranean currents of the *Saraswati*, my son. There is nothing to fear. Come and sit with me before we return to Baritun to give your sisters vigil. She caressed his face and spoke to him of the Hindu cycle of life.

"The soul is part of the limited being, the *Jiva*, and moves on when the body dies. It is imperishable. Our spirits will follow the bright path."

With those words, they ascended from the river, his mother chanting the *Ganga Mataki Jai*:

Glory, glory, all glory to you, O sanctifier of the world glory to you,
O Ganga, the sacred river of the gods. Victory to you,
O dweller among Shiva's locks!
Your bouncing and rippling waves are incomparably
beautiful.

From above the newly reconstructed road in Baritum—that passed the house of the Mehrases' closest friends, who had lovingly provided shelter for their orphaned daughters—Rimyi watched joyfully as Aaheli and Farha dug their small fingers into the just-poured asphalt.

"Bhai-ya, bhai-ya," they called out, sensing their beloved brother's presence in the steam and scent that rose from the restored surface.

And now, like Rimyi, they too possessed the wondrous ability to blow immense black bubbles.

Little Conversations

*The time has come...
to talk of many things
Of why the sea is boiling hot,
and whether pigs have wings.*
—Lewis Carroll

It all began when Leonard Myers asked his wife if he was the greatest love of her life. As was the case when he had previously asked the same question, she was reluctant to respond. So he rephrased it.

"Am I the person you care for more than anybody in the world?"

"Please don't go there again, Lenny. You know that's an unfair question," pleaded Elizabeth.

"Why? Either I am or I'm not. It's pretty simple."

"No it's not. You're asking me to quantify my feelings, and that's something I can't do. I love many people . . . our daughter, my parents. I love you all very much," replied Elizabeth with mounting irritation.

"That's a cop-out. We all love somebody best, and I would think you would love your life partner above all others."

"And you love me better than anyone?" challenged Elizabeth.

"Of course I do," responded Leonard . . . though only after a slight hesitation.

"Aha! You had to think about that for a second," retorted his wife.

"No I didn't," protested Leonard, leaving the kitchen before his wife could press the issue further.

* * *

However, later the same day Leonard could not keep from raising the topic again. Her indecisiveness had gnawed at him in the hours that followed their earlier conversation. He felt her answer was evasive, making him wonder just how deep her feelings for him actually ran. The more he considered the subject the more upset he became. *A wife should always love her husband the most. If she doesn't, it's because there's someone else, another man maybe*, he asserted, growing increasingly agitated.

"You have to love someone best . . . or at least more. So who is it?" he questioned Elizabeth, in a tone that had become sharp-edged.

"This is childish," she said, exasperated. "I told you I love you all, so why don't you leave it at that? I'm not going to say I have greater affection for you than I do for our child or others in my life."

"What others?" demanded Leonard, and Elizabeth gave out a loud groan.

"Okay, I love you better than anybody on Earth. Is that what you really want to hear?"

She rolled her eyes toward the ceiling.

"I don't believe you. You're just saying that to get out of telling me how you really feel," countered Leonard.

"Oh, my god! Are you for real? I can't believe we're having this discussion. You're so paranoid," snapped Elizabeth, turning and heading to the kitchen sink.

An awkward silence followed. Only then did Leonard say what was actually on his mind.

"There's someone else, right? Who is he?"

Elizabeth sighed, turning slowly back to Leonard.

"Have you lost your mind? Did you just ask me if I'm having an affair? This time you've taken it too far."

"Well, you won't answer a simple question about how you feel about me, so there has to be . . . ."

"Shut up!" yelled Elizabeth, throwing an oven mitt at him. "I think you need to see a professional. You have a serious reality problem."

"Me? You're the one with the reality problem. You have a great husband and you're screwing around on him."

"Holy mother of god! How do you come up with this stuff?" spit Elizabeth. "Okay, you're right. I'm having a torrid love affair with . . . with the *septic tank* guy."

"Finally, the truth. You *admit* to having an affair then?" shouted Leonard.

"That's it. I've had it with this ludicrous conversation. I'm not going to be a part of this nonsense. I'm out of here."

"Going to rendezvous with your boyfriend?"

"No. He's picking me up," replied Elizabeth, sarcastically.

As if on cue, a horn sounded and she went to the window.

"There he is now, in fact," said Elizabeth, tauntingly.

"Slut!" growled Leonard, and disappeared into the basement.

Elizabeth checked her hair in the hallway mirror, and went to greet her ride.

"Hi Liz," said her best friend, Julie. "Ready to hit the mall?"

"God, I feel like hitting something," replied Elizabeth, exhaling deeply.

"Uh, oh, trouble in paradise? Talk to me, girl."

"Mind if we're quiet for a while? I'm kind of talked out right now," asked Elizabeth.

As the car pulled away, Leonard unlocked the cellar cabinet that held his prized gun collection.

"Bitch," he mumbled over and over, as he took cartridges from a box.

* * *

When Elizabeth returned home three hours later, she found her husband sitting alone in the darkness of the living room.

"You're back," he said, softly. "Hope you had a good time."

"Yes, I did," replied Elizabeth, her voice flat.

"I have something for you," said Leonard rising from the couch, his hands concealed behind him.

"Really?" replied Elizabeth, nonchalantly.

"Yeah, you deserve this," answered Leonard, moving toward his wife and revealing what he had held out of sight.

"Oh, you *are* crazy!" blurted Elizabeth, as her husband handed her a single red rose.

"I'm sorry. I know you love me best," he said, contritely.

Elizabeth gave him a baleful look and then smiled and put her arms around him.

"Maybe," she whispered in his ear.

Leonard stiffened, his eyes moving in the direction of his shotgun that was hidden from view.

The momentary silence was broken by the voice of their eleven-year-old daughter, Lori.

"Hi, you guys," she called from the hallway. "I'm home."

Both parents greeted her warmly, breaking their embrace.

"Hey, it's my little girl, who loves me more than anyone in the world, right honey?" said Leonard, extending his arms toward her.

"I love you *both* better than anyone in the world," she replied, running toward them, her arms outstretched.

"But maybe me the most?" muttered Leonard, as his daughter hugged her mother and then him.

Again, Leonard's eyes drifted toward his concealed weapon.

While his daughter actually said nothing further, Leonard believed he heard her say, "Yes, I love you the *most*, daddy."

Lori Myers's imagined words were enough to make her father happy . . . *for a moment.*

People of Color

We hunt them for the beauty of their skins.
—Lord Tennyson

"I hate this look!" bemoaned Lionel Chesley, staring at his image in his car's rearview mirror on his way to work. *Purple just doesn't suit me*, he thought, although it had seemed fine when he chose it. Now he couldn't wait to transit to another shade.

The Purples were not his kind of people, although they did try to befriend him. They were just too snooty for his tastes. *Live and learn*, mumbled Lionel, thinking how he had screwed up before. Two years ago, his sisters convinced him to get in touch with his female side, so he went pink. What a disaster. The constant ribbing from his buddies nearly put him over the edge. Since the 2030s, dermal manipulation had gone from being a novel way to stand out from the crowd at parties and special events (like Halloween and Valentine's Day) to a means of declaring one's social predilections and even political affinities—blue for liberals, red for conservatives, and so on. The late Reverend Jesse Jackson believed skin colorization fulfilled the dream of his Rainbow Coalition movement.

"No longer is the world just black and white," he proclaimed on *Meet the Press*. "It's chartreuse, magenta, teal, ochre, and an endless array of other beautiful pigments. While there are many shades, we're all primary colors in God's eyes."

* * *

However, most users of colorizers—and they were legion—simply chose them to gain greater connection with like-minded people. This was born out by a recent survey that revealed the principle reason people transited was to achieve a greater feeling of belonging —a sense of membership in something special. Lionel estimated it would be a week before he could make the shift to what was called Gamboge—described by Wikipedia as "a spicy mustard color derived from a Cambodian tree." It was manufactured by Transhide, a brand unknown to him. For his current flesh tone, he had chosen Skintint. He had tried other colorizers. Huetone left him spotty and Tingeman streaked his forehead and arms. Skintint held its color for a solid month and then faded quickly, indicating the need to take another dose in order to retain or change pigmentation. The effect of the tablet was quick and reliable. Lionel hoped Transhide's product would be equally dependable. His closest friends had chosen gamboge because of its rarity.

"Don't know anybody with this shade. It's about as uncommon as you can get," boasted Adam.

That was true. Lionel could not recall seeing anyone else with that particular tint, and he could understand why. There was nothing appealing about it to him, but he didn't want to further alienate his pals. He had resisted the transition, and it had caused a rift between him and the two guys he'd known since childhood. So if it meant looking jaundiced to retain their friendship, then so be it. After all, it would only be for a month.

"It holds for three months. Then it fades over another three months," he was informed by Adam.

"And a dose costs the same as other colorizers, so it's like getting two doses for free," added Bryan.

"Jesus! You're talking six months looking like baby shit," groused Lionel.

"You should see how people react. They're like *'what the . . .?'*" said Adam. Covered in gamboge, he reminded Lionel of the famous movie android, C-3PO, with a severe liver ailment.

"I can see why," quipped Lionel. When it came time to blend with Adam and Brian, Lionel reluctantly took the pill while they cheered him on. Within twenty-four hours, his flesh looked like it had been dipped in a contaminated vat of French's Mustard. The reaction of his office mates was more extreme than he expected, and for several days they mostly avoided him. In exasperation, Lionel finally confronted his cohorts during a staff meeting.

"What's the matter with you guys? It's just a different colorizer. It's not contagious, for God sakes! I've seen some of you in pretty bizarre shades over the years."

"Yeah, but nothing as . . . as *weird* as that," said a woman adorned in one of the many pastels so popular at the moment.

"It just doesn't really meld with anything. Not what you'd call a complimentary or flattering hue. Kind of disturbing, even scary," added someone veneered in light red.

"Well, at least it's a bold statement. Not a bland or ordinary look. Nothing humdrum about it," snapped Lionel.

"Maybe a bit *too* different. Not very, ah . . . pleasing to the eye," commented his boss, also dyed in light red.

Despite his considerable effort to regain the amity of his colleagues and acquaintances, they remained disapproving. Lionel began to count the weeks until he could transit to a more acceptable flesh tone. He would even become a Pastel, which he hated, if it meant fitting in again. To his mounting despondency, the negative response to gamboge reached beyond his workplace. He and his similarly tinted companions soon discovered that they were not welcome in their usual haunts.

"We don't want your kind in here," said the bartender at a pub he'd been to many times. Then matters got worse when a Gamboge's car struck and killed a child. Although all the evidence pointed to it being an accident, his pigmentation was cited as a factor in the tragic mishap. A headline in the *Akron Times* read:

The driver of the car that killed the ten-year-old sported a rare tint known as gamboge—a colorizer prominent among members of the South American organ trafficking cartel, Permuta Humano, and other fringe groups throughout the Americas.

"Holy shit! What have you guys done to me? This tint is a curse. It not only looks freaky, but it's worn by body snatchers and kid killers," blurted Lionel.

"That guy didn't deliberately hit that kid. Poor bastard! He's being persecuted because of his tint," protested Adam.

"Yeah, it's guilt by color association," added Bryan, defensively.

"Whatever! I feel like an outcast. Nobody wants anything to do with us. We'll have to hide away like criminals until the color fades. I'm glad I don't live near my family. I wouldn't want them to see me this way," complained Lionel.

"Hey, man, we are what we are. They say color is just skin deep, right? Why should we be ostracized because of the shade of our flesh? People are nasty and ignorant," declared Brian, raising his clenched fist in the air.

Lionel and his friends stopped going to work. None of them could deal with the sudden snubbing and harsh looks they received. What is more, they began to feel physically threatened during outings. At one point in a supermarket parking lot, Adam was called a dirty Gam by a large Grey. For a moment he felt the man was going to attack him.

"I got the hell out of there fast. Guy was mean looking. Spit at my car as I drove past him," reported Adam, when he returned to Lionel's apartment. All three friends had decided to camp out at his place until the situation eased or their color faded.

"So we're dirty Gams, now? Why the hell did I listen to you guys? Purple was better than this. Shit, even pastel would be great compared to *gamboge*. Even the name sucks. Sounds like garbage and looks like it, too. Maybe that's why we're being treated like trash. I hated this color to begin with," complained Lionel, rubbing at his forearm as if his doing so might remove the loathsome tincture.

* * *

Disdain for Gams, as they had become widely known, continued to mount, much to the alarm of Lionel and his two best friends. Television news fanned the foment with frequent reports that cast the minority in an unfavorable light. Accounts sensationalized the alleged misdeeds of Gamboges. To believe the media, the tiny gamboge population was solely responsible for the growing urban blight and the significant rise in crime. Some officials interviewed by the press depicted Gams as lazy, immoral, and stupid.

"Why would anyone choose to colorize their skin with gamboge? That right there is an indication of the debased nature of these people," declared an Arizona congressman, who proposed that Gams be rounded up to prevent them from re-administering the colorizer and further jeopardizing society.

"The world has gone mad. This is so unreasonable. How could people single out a certain color as the root of all evils? It makes no sense at all. We're no different than anybody else. How can someone's skin tone make him subhuman?" decried Lionel.

* * *

Weeks dragged by as Lionel and his chums remained hidden from public view, only venturing out at night and in disguise to get food and other necessities. Meanwhile, the situation for Gamboges continued to deteriorate. They had become the object of every tinted and untinted person's animosity. To be a Gamboge was to be the lowest of all human life forms. For reasons beyond Lionel's comprehension, the world had decided to despise him and those like him. Two months into his gamboge colorization, Adam and Brian began to return to their original skin tones. This was reassuring, but as they regained their original pigment over the coming weeks, they too began to treat Lionel as if he were something to be scorned. Conflicts ensued and one morning they were gone. Lionel wondered if he were the last of his kind on earth, but the news reports indicated he was not. Other Gamboges existed but were being hunted down and incarcerated. Many were being used as forced labor until their skin pigmentation transited. Even then they were stigmatized for having been Gamboges and reduced to function in the lowest rungs of society. Lionel kept a close watch at the calendar and with a week to go before he was scheduled to begin fading, his friends knocked on his apartment door expressing their concern for him.

"We have some food. You must be starving. Let us in, Lionel. We're sorry for acting the way we did," said Adam, contritely.

"I'm fine," growled Lionel, his anger for his one-time friends still raw.

"Hey, we've been buddies forever. Don't drop us because we acted like jerks one time. We were just scared," added Brian.

"Scared of a dirty Gam like me, huh? What was I going to do to you guys? You had just transited from gamboge yourselves and you acted like I was something from an alien world," replied Lionel, his head pressed against the door.

"Look, we were being stupid. Saw all those TV reports about Gams . . . I mean Gamboges, acting like freaks. We just lost perspective. Come on, let us in, Lionel. You know us. Jeez . . .," said Adam, beseechingly.

"I'm still pissed at you guys," replied Lionel, his ire diminishing.

"We don't blame you, man. Let us in. You need to eat something, and I bet you'd like some company, too," pleaded Adam. After a pause, Lionel unlocked the door, and, as soon as he did, both Adam and Brian barged in. They were accompanied by several other men of varying colors.

"What's going on?" shouted Lionel, as he was seized and dragged from his apartment.

"Sorry, Lionel. They made us do it. They hate former Gamboges, too," offered Adam, with a pained expression.

"You're just a lowly, good for nothing Gam, and you shouldn't be allowed to live with normal people!" barked a member of the hostile mob.

Lionel was carried from the building to a nearby tree.

"String up the friggin' Gam!" yelled someone, and the rest of the group echoed his sentiment.

"What are you doing? I'm one of you . . . a human being. Just another person of color. Look, I'm about to transit. I'll be neutral soon," pleaded Lionel, as a noose was place around his neck.

"You ain't transiting nowhere. Once a Gam always a Gam," responded a burly Aubergine, heaving the end of the rope over a thick tree branch.

"Please don't do this! Give me time to change color," begged Lionel.

"Okay, guys, grab the end of the rope and pull," directed a Malachite. As

Lionel was hoisted from the ground, words from a fabled speech rang in his ears:

I have a dream that one day we'll live in a nation that will not judge us by the color of our skin but by the content of our character.

Lionel's body remained dangling from the tree until it returned to its original ebony tone.

Incredulous

The woman struck by the speeding car

stared back at her severed legs

as if looking into an aquarium

filled with iridescent jellyfish.

The Forcing House

With them the Seed of Wisdom did I sow,
And with mine own hand wrought to make it grow.
—Edward Fitzgerald

In the small village of Dewsbury, England, the harsh winter of 1878 kept the ground frozen and snow-covered until early May. The lateness of the spring growing season had severely taxed the resources of Neville Laarman. His greenhouse was barren since the prolonged cold prevented him from producing the flowers necessary to support himself and his family. As soon as the weather broke, he hurriedly seeded his pots with fast growing Zinnias, Nasturtiums, Marigolds, Cosmos, and Alyssum, among a host of others.

In addition to the usual seeding, Neville buried the gametes he had purchased months earlier from an individual on his way to Leeds to give a lecture. The stranger claimed to be a noted botanist who had developed an extraordinary blossom from a blend of *Roridula, Heterophylia, Drosera, Cephalotus, Tonala, Konda, Chrysolepis,* and *Drosophyllum*—flora totally unfamiliar to Neville, who knew his flowering plants better than most men.

"*Omorfi Gigantas Loulouthi*—beautiful giant flower, to the uninitiated, sir. If that is difficult to remember, simply refer to it by its creator's moniker,

Maskelyne," he said, with a courtly bow.

The well-dressed gentleman had a fine sketch of the bloom, whose large variegated petals featured several vibrant colors that appeared to rise from the paper. Although the cost of the packet containing the exotic admixture was exorbitant, Neville was confident his investment would be recouped manifold. *Surely his customers would be as dazzled by the rare flower as he was*, he thought.

But the expenditure had compounded the hardship caused by the protracted winter. His wife, Eliza, complained about the dwindling of provisions needed to feed their three children. The situation was made all the more dire due to the medical needs of their nine-year-old son, a dwarf named Joshua, whose deformed spine caused him constant pain and difficulties walking. Neville often carried his crippled child to the greenhouse to distract him from the hardships of his young existence. The boy's mood invariably improved as he watched his father fill and seed the terracotta pots. They would sing, and occasionally Neville would hoist Joshua to his shoulders and dance a Slip jig until his son's back pain required he be returned to his special chair.

"That was fun, father. Thank you," Joshua would say gratefully, and his father could not look at him because of the tears in his eyes.

There was nothing Neville would not do or give to see his only son healthy and happy. It caused him unbearable sorrow to know that Joshua would live out what remained of his life so terribly afflicted.

* * *

Although the snow gradually melted, it remained unseasonably cold, and Neville knew his seedlings were in peril. In an attempt to insure their growth, he constructed a makeshift wood stove to keep the frigid air from killing the precious roots he prayed were forming in their containers. Before retiring for his short night's sleep—usually no more than four hours—he filled the stove with enough logs to heat the nursery until his return the next morning.

Not long after Neville slipped into bed next to his wife and fell into a deep sleep, a hard Polar gust that had battered the area all winter long caused a tree limb to strike the greenhouse stove's flue, which was vented through an opening in the glass roof. This caused the damper to come apart, showering embers on the pallet holding the pots with the special seeds purchased at so high a price. Soon the wood table caught fire.

Fate intervened, stirring Neville from a disturbing dream. He awoke with his heart pounding, fearing that something awful had happened and very quickly realizing that it had. Luckily, the fire had not spread far when he reached the greenhouse, and he was able to douse the flames with buckets of leftover snow.

Despite his relief that his business had not burned to the ground, he soon realized the costly Maskelynes had been a casualty of the blaze. All that remained in the charred pots was ash. Neville was deeply distressed as he mixed new soil with the slag of his failed venture and placed what common seeds remained in it. Although he had slept only a little that night, he knew he would not be able to go back to sleep. Thoughts of his bad fortune would prevent him from doing so. Instead, he cleaned the debris from the fire and fixed the stove's flue. When the sun rose, he returned to the house for breakfast.

"Are you all right, Neville?" asked his wife, as he slumped into a kitchen chair.

He had not told Eliza about buying the Maskelyne seeds, because he knew she would raise valid objections. *She would have been right, too,* he thought, as he sipped his tea. *We would be far better off now with the money.*

"Just a little fire from the stove. Nothing of significance lost," he replied, knowing he was lying, since something of potentially tremendous significance had, indeed, been lost.

"Go to bed for a while. You need rest or you will get sick," urged Eliza, and Neville heeded her advice.

"Maybe for an hour," he answered, rising wearily from his seat and leaving the kitchen.

* * *

The unsettling nightmare that had been interrupted by his sudden awakening hours before returned. In it, his family was being sent away from him on a train, which he was kept from boarding, despite his valiant attempts to do so. As the train began to depart for its unknown destination, he woke shaken.

"Only two hours, but perhaps you feel better, love?" asked Eliza as she entered the bedroom. "There's porridge and sausage. Please eat before you go back out."

"Yes, I'm hungry. Thank you," answered Neville, taking his wife's hand and gently kissing it.

Neville felt slightly better by the time he reached the greenhouse, but when his eyes landed on the pots that once held the promise of a brighter future, he stopped in his tracks. Rising before him were fully bloomed Zinnias, Marigolds, and Cosmos.

"Impossible!" he blurted, as he made a closer inspection of the startling growths.

Only hours earlier he had seeded those same pots, yet somehow the seedlings had grown to maturity in that brief time. He examined the pots carefully to ascertain if they were the same ones he had filled. They were. For a moment he feared he might be imagining things. He sat for several minutes staring at the miraculous flowers, and during that time, he thought he saw them growing even further. *The Maskelyne. Could it be the ashes of the Maskelyne?* wondered Neville, amazed by the possibility.

Two of the twelve pots that had contained the special seed had been left unfilled, and Neville collected their burnt contents, placing them in a leather pouch. To validate the apparent bizarre effect of the ash, he mixed some of it in the soil of another pot and placed Nasturtium seeds in it. He then set out to the market to purchase on credit a few food items requested by his wife. When he returned three hours later, gigantic red, yellow, and orange blossoms hung on long stems from the pot.

"Incredible," he mumbled, clutching the pouch containing the miraculous compound. A thought then occurred to him. Could it do for his son what it did for the plants? Would it give him growth? In only a moment, he determined to ascertain the answer. He would mix the ash in Joshua's food and hope the Maskelyne sediment would perform its magic on his stunted child. Neville felt it was worth any risk the enigmatic compound might pose if it brought relief to his child's suffering.

Again, Neville decided against revealing his plan to his wife. She was a very sensible, if not overly cautious, woman, who would surely be against experimenting with their only son. He hoped his actions would not prove her right. Although he did feel some trepidation about his son ingesting the mysterious substance, he felt it was worth the risk if it resulted in a better life for his cherished offspring.

* * *

At the midday meal, Neville poured a small amount of the mixture in

Joshua's milk. After consuming a large bowl of cock-a-leekie, a special stew made by his wife, he returned to the greenhouse, and again noted the continued growth of the Nasturtiums. By then, their tendrils reached the ground, and the Zinnias, Cosmos, and Marigolds were twice the size they had been. He quickly informed his neighbors and townsfolk of his extraordinary flowers, and by nightfall, he had sold them to enthusiastic customers for an impressive sum. Encouraged by the results, he mixed the Maskelyne ash in a batch of soil and filled several more pots with seeds.

The next morning he rose well before dawn and dashed excitedly to the greenhouse. To his pleasure, a burst of vividly colored plants greeted him.

"Thank you, thank you," he mumbled, his eyes cast upward.

Apparently the voluptuous petals had attracted rodents as well, because Neville noticed chomp marks on some. As the sun rose, he arranged a row of tables outside of the greenhouse on which to display his resplendent merchandise. As he stood staring admiringly at his wares, his wife shouted for him to come to the house. When he entered, he found Eliza weeping.

"What's the matter?" he asked, and she responded by pointing in the direction of the kitchen.

When Neville entered the cookery, he found standing next to the sink a youngster who looked vaguely familiar to him.

"Who are . . .?" he sputtered, and then he realized it was Joshua. "Oh Lord, is it you?"

"Yes, father. Look how I have grown."

Indeed, the boy stood at least a foot taller and completely erect.

"How can this be?" sobbed Eliza. "It is the work of God. A miracle!"

"Yes, it is a miracle. A wonderful gift," said Neville, embracing his son.

"No pain, father, and look how straight I stand," said Joshua, with a broad smile.

OF NIGHT AND LIGHT

* * *

In the days that followed, the Laarmans celebrated their exceptional fortune. Thanks to sales of the miracle flowers, their finances improved dramatically, and they were able to pay off their creditors and purchase much-needed goods for their household and children. Neville's nursery had become the talk of Dewsbury and the surrounding areas, and the demand for his plants nearly exceeded his ability to produce them. Miraculously, the ashes seemed to regenerate themselves as his pouch never emptied. Everything was as good as he could possibly imagine.

Neville's only concern was his son's continuing growth spurts. By now he had exceeded the height of his mother and was closing in on his father's height. *What if he continues to grow unabated?* wondered Neville, who had ceased putting the Maskelyne residue in Joshua's food after two applications. Still, he was delighted that his son no longer suffered from his affliction and believed he would stop growing at a reasonable size.

"Father, I think I'll soon be able to ride *you* on my shoulders," remarked Joshua, as he worked along with his father in the greenhouse.

"That would be wonderful," answered his father, secretly hoping it would never come to pass.

In the middle of the night, Neville was awakened by a noise coming from the greenhouse. The fire in the wood stove cast a faint glow, and he thought he detected a shadow. *Was there someone in there trying to discover the reason his plants grew so robustly?* he considered.

As he opened the greenhouse door, a loud squeal accosted him, and a table containing plants toppled over.

"Who's there? Get out of there!" threatened Neville, as he moved forward cautiously.

Another strident squeal filled the air, and then a large object appeared at the far end of the greenhouse.

"God!" screamed Neville, and then he was attacked, his head torn from his body.

In the moonlight, the dark contours of the mammoth rats could be seen scurrying from the greenhouse toward the sleeping village.

Making Light

Chaos, illumined by flashes of lightning
—Oscar WIlde

The Centennial Light had cast its soft glow in a California firehouse for nearly 110 years. While an amazing and wondrous thing to see, it inspired the ire of many who manufactured and sold light bulbs.

Complained Nathan Zelnick, Jr., co-owner of Zelnick Lighting Outlet, "We'd be out of business if bulbs lasted that long. Imagine if every product had an unlimited lifespan? This country's economy would be up shit creek, and nobody would want that. Yet everyone wants a bulb like the Centennial. They don't know what they're wishing for."

Nathan saw red every time he had to deal with the question of why modern light bulbs had such limited longevity compared to the celebrated Centennial's eternal glow. He speculated that his store's two-block proximity to Fire Station 6 that housed the seemingly immortal four-watt, carbon filament lamp made his business the biggest target of consumer skepticism and dissatisfaction.

"If that bulb can last forever, why can't GE make another one? After-all, it made the darn thing," was a frequent customer complaint.

"It's a fluke," responded Nathan defensively. "Just one of those weird things that happens and can't be duplicated. That's why they call it a miracle.

Besides, the Shelby Electric Company made it . . . *not* GE."

"Well, these bulbs you sell are built to blow out sooner than they should. It's all part of that obso . . . something strategy of big business designed to keep our pockets empty and theirs full."

"Hey, it keeps my store running and a roof over your head. You should be thankful for that!" snapped Nathan. "Besides, I don't make them. I just sell them."

For twenty-seven years, Nathan had run the store with his older brother, Sam. When his father died, despite being younger, Nathan had been put in charge of the business, due to Sam's attention deficit disorder and hyperthyroidism that made it difficult for him to deal with customers. Most of Sam's time was spent in the back room dealing with inventory, and even then Nathan had to keep a wary eye on him for fear his brother would miscount product, resulting in insufficient stock. It was an all-too-common problem, and despite his affection for Sam, Nathan often wished he could be rid of him. Still, as neither man was married, they depended on each other's company when the store closed for the day and they retreated to the apartment above it that they shared.

Conversation between the brothers did not amount to much and usually ended with Nathan complaining about the Centennial light bulb—the singular bane of his existence. It was during one such lament that Sam proposed a solution.

"Let's just sneak over to the station when they're out on a call and shoot the bulb with your BB gun."

"I've been sorely tempted to do just that. I'm so sick of patrons telling me we're cheating them because of that damn bulb," responded Nathan staring out of the window toward the firehouse.

Eventually, he decided to take action. He'd had enough of his customers' complaints and was close to bursting with frustration. Something had to be done and quickly. It was either that or shut down the business, and he was not about to do that because of what he considered a freak of nature.

* * *

That night Nathan and Sam practiced shooting the BB gun in the building's basement. Sam was the sharp shooter of the two, but Nathan had declared himself the one who would take out the pesky bulb.

"Why you?" complained Sam. "I'm better. You missed the lampshade three times."

"Because I've been the one tormented by that bulb. Not you. You haven't had to deal with all the snide comments from customers. I have, and I'm going to enjoy payback."

The Zelnicks settled on the following Sunday night to execute their plan because the neighborhood would be at its quietest. They would wait for the firehouse alarm to ring and when the trucks and firefighters were gone, they would take action. However, they had to wait through three Sundays for the alarm to finally sound at the convenient time. When it did, it was at 3 o'clock in the morning, and Nathan could not get Sam out of bed. So he threw on his clothes and headed over to the firehouse alone, clutching the Daisy BB gun he'd been given as a kid.

As expected, the streets were deserted and the firehouse doors open and unattended. He carefully approached the building making certain nobody was about. At the entrance, he took aim at the Centennial bulb and squeezed the trigger. The fired pellet glanced off the wall a foot from the dangling incandescent. His next shot was on target, but rather than shattering the bulb, the BB shot caused a blinding flash and when the glow subsided the bulb was still intact.

Nathan was perplexed and wondered if there was some kind of shield around the light to protect it. After scouting the area again for anyone who might see him or hear the BB gun, he moved inside the firehouse to a point directly under the bulb. He then took careful aim and shot at it. Again, a brilliant blast of light issued forth from the bulb. It was so bright it took Nathan's eyes several moments to return to normal. Spooked by what had happened, he dashed out of the firehouse towards home.

What the hell? he wondered as he opened the entrance to the store on the way to the apartment. As soon as he was inside he sensed something was wrong. Then he realized that the display lamps that were always on were dark. When he tried their switches, nothing happened.

"A damn fuse," muttered Nathan, who headed to the basement to check the circuit breaker. The switches were all in the right position indicating power was still on. He returned to the display floor figuring the plugs must have come loose, but to his surprise, they were snug in their outlets.

When Nathan climbed the stairs back to his apartment above the store, he found Sam watching television in their dark living room.

"Do the lights work?" he inquired, and his brother said he didn't know.

"Well, try the lamp, for cripes sakes!" snapped Nathan, who then tried the switch on the lamp himself.

"Nothing! How the hell can that be? The TV is on. It doesn't make sense. Look, the electric wall clock is on too."

"What's the matter?" asked his brother, his eyes still fixed on the television.

"I don't know. Something weird is going on."

Nathan's eyes then drifted to the window.

"The street light is out," he observed, walking to the window and peering out. "Hey, none of them are on. There are no lights coming from any place at all.

Must be a blackout, but how can that be if the power is still on for the TV and clock?"

"Wonder if the Centennial Light is still on," said Sam.

"Good thought. I'll go check," replied Nathan, who dashed back down the stairs and out of the door.

In the darkness of the fire station a tiny glow emanated from the ceiling.

"I'll be damned," muttered Nathan, who then heard the returning fire trucks and ran away.

On his return home, Nathan noticed that no lights were evident in any direction, not even from houses in the distant hills.

"Look," said Sam when Nathan entered the apartment. "They're reporting a blackout all over the state."

Nathan watched as a shadowy figure from a dim studio reported that all illumination devices appeared to be effected.

"Power exists for everything except lights. This is already causing significant problems throughout the state, especially for hospitals and other critical service agencies."

"Hey, was the bulb still on?" inquired Sam, chomping on a Frito.

"Yeah, it was," answered Nathan, with a far-off look in his eyes. "Maybe I caused the blackout when I tried to shoot out the bulb. Something really weird happened. Every time I tried to kill it, there was an explosion of light. It almost blinded me."

"Maybe it didn't want to be shut off," commented Sam.

"Jeez, c'mon, Sammy. Are you saying it has a mind of its own?"

"Who knows? Nobody can explain why it's stayed on for over a century, right? Maybe it's an alien instrument. Could be they put it here to observe us," offered Sam, his eyes bouncing between his brother and the television.

"Now, that's really dumb!" spouted Nathan.

"And maybe they know you tried to shoot it out?" continued Sam. "Man, they could be coming for you right now."

"Why do I even try to have a sensible conversation with someone who has watched *Close Encounters* over a hundred times," responded Nathan, disgustedly.

"One hundred eighteen times to be exact, little brother."

Nathan's attention returned to the television reporter who was giving an update on the worsening situation.

"According to authorities, the blackout is not limited to California. In fact, it has spread across the country."

"You really did it now, Natty," interjected Sam.

"Shut up and listen!" barked Nathan.

"FEMA reports that lights are out in every state," reported the newscaster's voice over a satellite map of the country shrouded in darkness. "Strangely, however, it seems that the famous Centennial Light in the Livermore-Pleasanton fire station remains on."

"You see, Nathan. It is from outer space," gloated Sam.

"Shush!!" responded Nathan.

"Here it is folks. A live picture of the Centennial Light from the station's bulbcam."

The image of the solitary bulb gave Nathan the shivers. He felt as if it were a malevolent eye cast solely on him. *What horrible event had he set in motion*, he wondered?

"There are now reports that both Canada and Mexico also are in the dark. This may well be a global phenomenon. Furthermore, it appears that any attempt to generate light fails. We have reports that flashlights and car headlights do not work and even candles will not ignite."

As the moments passed and reports of light outages become more widespread, Nathan grew convinced that his attempt to destroy the Centennial Light was behind what was happening.

"I bet we're being invaded. It's an alien beacon guiding them to our planet," said Sam, pacing back and forth in front of the television.

"I better call the police and let them know what I did," muttered Nathan.

"Probably going to harvest us or make us their slaves."

"For God sakes, shut up, Sam!" bellowed Nathan, as he dialed 911 on his cellphone.

After several busy signals, his call reached the emergency operator and he detailed his attempt to shoot out the ancient bulb, suggesting that his action was the likely cause of the blackout. The 911 operator asked for his name and address and hung up.

"So, are they coming to arrest you?" inquired Sam.

"I don't know. I have the feeling they thought I was a crank," responded Nathan.

"Maybe we should go to the station and try to knock out the bulb again. The fire trucks just went on a call. Bet they're busy with the blackout," observed Sam.

"Why would we do that? It's probably what caused this mess in the first place!" snapped Nathan.

"What if your old Daisy wasn't powerful enough to shoot out the bulb? We could try to hit it with something . . . maybe a rock or brick. Could be once it's out, the aliens will not be able to follow through with their plan."

"What plan? This whole thing is crazy. I don't know. Maybe you're right. Something sure as hell is odd about that light," admitted Nathan.

"Well, let's do it," said Sam, with the resolve of a military commando.

The brothers crept down the dark stairs and furtively walked along the equally dark street to the firehouse. As they stood before its open doors, they could see the Centennial Light as it glowed ominously.

"Here, try this," said Sam, handing his brother a rock the size of a baseball.

Nathan chucked it at the bulb missing it by a couple of feet.

"Sandy Koufax you're not. Let me try," said Sam, winding up to throw another fist-size rock.

His attempt was on target but caused such a blast of light that they flinched and stepped back. When the burst of brightness subsided, the bulb still shone intact.

"Hey, what are you guys doing?" shouted someone behind them. "You're not authorized to be in here."

A man in full firefighter garb approached them.

"That bulb is behind the blackout," blurted Sam, pointing upward.

"What?" asked the fireman, now standing just inches from the distraught brothers.

"We're certain that light has something to do with what's going on, and I think I started the whole thing," said Nathan, on the verge of tears.

"What do you mean?"

"A few hours ago, I tried to shoot out the bulb, and right after that everything went dark."

"Why would you try to do that?" asked the fireman, removing his helmet. "It's an icon . . . very historic."

"It's been a royal pain in the ass. Customers keep saying we're cheating them with short life bulbs," explained Nathan.

"Hey, I know you. You guys run Zelnick's down the street, right?"

"Look, we think if the bulb is put out things will return to normal," offered Nathan.

"Yeah, and then the aliens won't attack," added Sam.

"Aliens? What are you talking about? You guys lose your marbles?"

"Look, you can't destroy it," said Sam, chucking another rock at the Centennial light.

His aim was perfect and once again created a tremendous blast of light that caused the men to recoil.

"What the hell . . .!" blurted the fireman covering his eyes.

"You see. It's not of this world," said Sam. "It's an alien mechanism placed here in advance of an invasion."

"Jeez, it's strange, but I don't know about any alien invasion. That's pretty out there, pal."

"Well, it's got some connection with what's happening. I'm sure of that," said Nathan.

"Maybe it does," responded the firefighter, nervously rubbing his forehead.

* * *

A crowd began to gather outside of the firehouse having witnessed the blasts of light from the Centennial Light over the bulbcam. Several police cars soon appeared followed by the FBI and other officials. The media were hot on their heels to the scene. By late afternoon, the world was tuned into the Livermore firehouse and people were growing convinced that the bulb was the source of the mayhem. Global hysteria began to build over the fear that the blackout was caused by malevolent forces not of this world.

It was decided that the Centennial bulb had to be destroyed, and several ideas to do so were quickly suggested by the police and military. The first involved the use of high-powered rifles, but they failed to extinguish the light. Next the area was cleared and heavy artillery brought in. Several rounds were fired, resulting in the destruction of most of the firehouse, but when the smoke cleared, the Centennial bulb continued to glow from the electrical cord that hung perilously from a cross beam.

"We'll have to bomb it," said General Gillespie of the state's Army National Guard. "That's the only thing that will do it in, and it will have to be a substantial barrage to insure the job gets done. Of course, there will be collateral damage. Several blocks will be leveled, so let's start evacuation procedures."

"That will destroy our store!" exclaimed Nathan.

"Wait!" shouted Sam. "I have an idea. Let me try to unscrew it from the socket."

"What a novel idea," responded the general, sarcastically.

"Well, no one has tried that."

"You want to be electrocuted?" growled the general.

"No, Sam," said Nathan. "Let me try to unscrew it. I started this thing."

"Well, go ahead if you're crazy enough to try it," conceded the general. "Get this guy a ladder, and I want everybody to get way back. Have the ambulance ready to remove his crispy remains. You got something this guy can use so he doesn't burn himself when he makes contact with the light?"

"We got a UV-glove in the kitchen," replied a fireman.

"You mean the one they advertise on TV?" asked the general.

"Yes sir."

"Great product. Go get it."

When the ladder was in place, Nathan climbed it slowly. *I'll never make it*, he thought, as he neared the Centennial bulb.

Sam held his breath as he stood with the crowd several hundred feet away.

I'm dead at any moment, thought Nathan, as he reached the bulb. His hand trembled as he began to twist the bulb from its socket. To his great relief there was no blinding burst of light. After two turns, it went out, prompting a huge sigh from the crowd.

At the moment the Centennial went dark, the lights in what remained of the decimated firehouse came on, as did the streetlights. These were greeted with loud cheers from the assembled crowd.

"Whaddya know," said General Gillespie, shaking his head in amazement. "All we had to do was unscrew the goddamn thing to prevent this chaos."

As a safety precaution, several other long-running light bulbs, including the Eternal Light in Fort Worth, Texas, the Gasnick Bulb in New York City, and the Mangum Light in the Oklahoma town bearing its name, were unscrewed and destroyed.

Once again, the world was fully illuminated, but concern about the cause of the blackout lingered. Theories ranging from an alien invasion to a warning message from God filled the news for weeks after the blackout. But as with all stories, eventually interest faded and life returned to normal.

* * *

For Nathan, the quality of his existence vastly improved, not only because he was proclaimed a hero for re-illuminating the world, but also because his customers now held the belief that built-in obsolescence was a highly desirable element in the products he sold. It was not until a year had passed that Nathan noticed that none of the bulbs in his store had burned out.

A Sticky Yellow Place

Half hidden from the eye . . .
shining in the sky.
—William Wordsworth

There was something unsettling in the back of twelve-year-old Sandra's closet. At times she could actually smell it, but she was the only one who could. She first discovered its presence when looking for the mate to a pair of sneakers. Groping around in the deep recesses of her closet, she touched an object that made her recoil. At first Sandra thought it was a cobweb, but when she looked at her hand she knew better. Whatever she had encountered left a sticky yellow residue on her fingers rather than the delicate threads of a spider's handiwork.

She reported the incident to her mother, Kerri Giles, who found nothing after removing everything the enclosure contained. Despite this, Sandra remained unconvinced that the space was clear and decided then and there to never again reach that far in. Whatever she had come in contact with could remain there unmolested as far as she was concerned. As time passed, however, with not a day going by that the episode left her thoughts, her resolve began to give way to curiosity. Sandra needed to know if she had just imagined the disturbing event, because she wanted to put her doubt to rest once and for all.

Once Sandra decided to meet the situation head on, it took her awhile to muster the courage to probe the closet's innards. There was no way she was using her hand again, so she used her mother's yardstick to do the poking. Since the closet had no light, she also enlisted the aid of a flashlight to illuminate the mystery. When the time came to launch the expedition, Sandra locked the door to her room. She didn't want to be discovered by her mother, who had declared the whole thing a figment of her daughter's overactive imagination.

As soon as she opened the closet door, her nostrils were beset by a rancid odor that reminded her of the smell that sometimes rose from the garbage disposal. It caused Sandra to crinkle her nose as she leaned slightly into the closet with the tools of her search. When the yardstick came in contact with something malleable, Sandra thought it was her pair of Uggs, but the beam of the flashlight revealed otherwise. There in the inner sanctum of the closet was a slimy pulsating object attached to the wall. It made Sandra scream and jump backward. When she caught her breath, she slammed the door shut.

* * *

Sandra refused to reopen the closet for several days. When her mother asked why she hadn't changed her clothes, she tearfully revealed the reason.

"Not that again, honey. There's nothing in there. I emptied it out and showed you."

"I know, but there's really something in there," protested Sandra.

"What is it that you think is in your closet?" asked Mrs. Giles, attempting to placate her nearly hysterical child.

"I don't know. It's a yucky, stinky thing," answered Sandra.

"We checked it for smells, and we couldn't detect any. You know that, sweetheart."

"Please, mom, check it again. There's something awful in there, and I won't open the door any more. I don't care if I have to wear these clothes forever," stammered Sandra.

"Okay, when your father comes home, we'll take another look. Maybe it needs to be repainted. I know the walls are chipping and scaling in all the closets. That quake, or whatever it was a few weeks ago, has left this house falling apart," offered Sandra's mother.

When Larry Giles arrived from work, his wife informed him of the situation, and he agreed to conduct a thorough renovation of all the house's closets, starting with Sandra's.

"Lord knows what else needs attention in this place, but we'll start in your room and work from there," observed Mr. Giles, removing his tie.

While her parents emptied it, Sandra stood at a distance behind them fearing what may be discovered. They carefully piled her clothes on her bed, and stacked her shoes atop a chest containing her collection of My Little Pony and Barbie dolls.

"There ... *nothing*. Empty as Mother Hubbard's cupboard," declared her father.

"See, Sandra. Come over and look. No yucky, stinky thing," announced Kerri Giles, smiling at her daughter consolingly.

Sandra moved toward the closet slowly. Indeed, it *was* empty as her parents claimed. *But how could that be? There was a horrible thing in there just a while ago. Where could it be now?* she wondered, her apprehension still high.

"I'll paint it tomorrow. Get rid of all those ugly cracks. Didn't realize how bad it was inside there. It's probably what you saw. No boogeyman, honey, just old dried up walls that need some Spackle and Dutch Boy. We'll leave the door open so it will air out," said Mr. Giles, exiting the room.

"Let's move your clothes off your bed, so you have room to sleep tonight, okay? And please put on something clean, Sandra. Maybe what you've been smelling is yourself," said her mother, only half joking.

* * *

Long after Sandra went to bed, she kept her eyes fixed on the open closet. Finally, as she was about to drift off, she thought she heard something coming from it . . . a raspy voice. Sandra pulled the covers over her head until she began to perspire. After several agonizing moments of silence, she heard her name called. When she dared to peek out from under the puff, she saw a soft glow inside the closet and a shadow move against its back wall.

"Sandra . . . Sandra. Come, Sandra," beckoned the unwelcome intruder.

Sandra leapt from the bed and ran from her room. She took refuge beneath the thick down comforter on the bed in the guest room, where she remained until she heard her mother calling for her in the morning. Sandra slipped from under the protective covers and met her mother in the hall.

"What were you doing in there?"

"I saw . . ." sputtered Sandra, deciding not to say anything about the voice in the closet.

"Saw what?" asked Mrs. Giles.

"Nothing . . . I just couldn't sleep in my bed, so I tried the one in the guest room," answered Sandra, her heart racing.

"Was it the closet? It was, wasn't it? You were afraid, huh? Well, daddy is going to take care of it today. It will be like new tonight, so that should help you get over this."

After breakfast, Larry Giles went to work on Sandra's closet filling in the wide cracks and double-coating it with white paint.

"Come in and see your new and improved closet, Sandy," called her father.

To her profound relief, it did appear new and improved, and most of all it seemed absent of any evidence that something awful had resided in it.

"I was going to paint it yellow, but I thought it would be easier for you to choose an outfit against a more neutral backdrop. How's that thinking, young lady?" said Mr. Giles, proudly.

"Great, daddy. I hate yellow anyway," Sandra assured her father.

"Oh, I thought you loved yellow."

"Not any more," replied Sandra, giving her father an appreciative hug.

Hey, what's this?" asked Mr. Giles, holding his daughter's wrist.

During the past two days, a rash had formed on Sandra's hand. At first it was small, but it quickly grew to cover most of her forearm, as well as her hand.

"I don't know," answered Sandra, scratching at it.

"Better not do that. It could spread. Have mom look at it. Doesn't look like poison ivy. Odd color . . . mustardy."

"I will," said Sandra to her father, as he removed a drop cloth and paint can from the revitalized closet and left her room.

* * *

Later in the afternoon, when the paint had dried, Sandra hung her cloths and carefully organized her shoes in the refurbished closet, but her anxiety had not left her entirely. In fact, the more time she spent in the space, the more she sensed the presence of the unknown entity that had seemingly possessed it. By the time she was finished storing her wardrobe, she was certain the demon––for that is how she now thought of it—had reclaimed the rear wall of the closet.

At supper, Sandra's parents noticed that the rash on her arm now extended to her neck.

"We'll take you to the dermatologist tomorrow, Sandy," said her father, and her mother implored her to stop scratching the rash.

"It's itchy," replied Sandra. "And I think it smells, too."

"I don't smell anything, honey, but if you keep digging at it, it'll become infected," observed Kerri Giles.

Sandra excused herself from the dinner table and returned to her room. As soon as she entered it, she noticed the closet door that had been tightly shut was open. *It's out*, she thought, scanning her room, but then the closet door slowly shut. *I can't stay here . . . I can't stay in this room*, she repeated to herself. She turned and dashed to the bedroom door, only to find it locked.

"Sandra . . .," came the unearthly voice from the closet. "Sandra, there is nothing to fear. Nothing to fear at all."

As the muffled words continued to flow from behind the closet door, she suddenly felt less afraid, even soothed.

"We are already one. From the moment you touched me we became the same. Our atoms have united, and soon we'll be able to leave. The transmigration will soon take place. It has taken so long . . . so *very* long."

Sandra listened intently and was directed to enter the closet whose door crept open.

"No longer in exile on this wretched planet. My sentence has been served. Liberation is mine. Come, Sandra. The cycle nears completion."

"Yes," said Sandra, entering the closet, "the cycle nears completion."

* * *

After calling her daughter to breakfast three times, Kerri Giles went to her room and tapped on the door. When there was no answer, she entered it.

"Honey, it's time to get up," she whispered affectionately as she tugged the covers from her daughter.

Sandra's father dropped his cup of freshly poured coffee when he heard the horrific scream coming from the second floor. He climbed the stairs three at a time and arrived at his daughter's bedroom where he found his wife standing over what looked like giant, flesh colored amoeba.

"Jesus!" he yelled. "What is that?"

As he reached his wife's side, the stench rising from the quivering mass caused the contents of his stomach to explode past his lips.

"She's in there!" cried Mrs. Giles. "Look, I can see Sandra's face!"

As they leaned into the foreign object, it sprang open ripping them from where they stood and sucking them inside. A moment later, it rose from the bed and swept out of the window, disappearing into the cloudless sky.

My Secret Tanzania

Come live with me, and be my love
And we will some new pleasures prove.
—John Donne

The Hotel Talapia lay at the base of a steep escarpment atop which giant vultures perched and squawked mournfully. Occasionally a wispy cloud covered its peak and further heightened the exotic aura of Tanzania's westernmost township. Mwanza was the country's third-highest populated community and sat on the southwestern edge of Lake Victoria. It offered visitors a myriad of distinct aromas and solitary sights that made Professor Paul Stanton feel as if he'd been transported to another planet. Although he had traveled widely, no place appeared more otherworldly to him, and it made him giddy with curiosity and excitement.

The State Department had sent him to the sub-equatorial country to instruct female Non Government Organizations (NGOs) on how to develop their own small businesses. It was his first time working for the government in any capacity, except as an army draftee. His regular position was professor of finance at Cantor College in Northern Vermont. A close friend and longtime co-author, Curtis Hill, had worked for the United States International Entrepreneurial Initiative (USIEI) several times and had recommended Paul for an assignment after Paul had asked (more like pleaded) for him to do so.

One week after Paul's semester ended, he landed in Dar es Salaam and was met by an embassy aide.

"Welcome to Dar, Mr. Stanton. I'm John Halloran. How was your trip?"

Paul reported he had been unable to sleep on either leg of the trip from Boston, which meant he'd been up for 48 hours.

"You must be exhausted. I'll take you to your hotel. Later, if you're up to it, you're welcome to join a group of us for dinner at Nyumba...great Ethiopian food.

"That sounds good. Haven't had anything worth swallowing since I left the States," replied Paul, eager to immerse himself in the local community as soon as possible.

"Later they're showing a Jackie Chan movie at the Marine base. Screen is outside under the stars. You might get a kick out of it if you're still awake," offered Halloran, pulling up to the New Africa Hotel. "They have a pretty decent bar. What say I meet you there in three hours? Gives you time to settle in and maybe take a nap."

Paul found the accommodations comparable to a Motel 5 back home, but he rated the view from his room as at least a ten. It overlooked the city's busy harbor and its palm tree laden waterfront park. Directly across from the hotel stood a prominent brick church, crowned by a gold cross that shimmered in the bright sunlight. In its courtyard, which he could see from his eleventh floor window, a wedding reception appeared underway. The bride and groom looked like they could be from anywhere, attired as they were in a black tux and white wedding gown with a sprawling train. Paul was somewhat disappointed that they were adorned in Western rather than traditional African attire.

After taking a shower, he tried to nap but found he was too wound up. He turned on the television remote and watched CNN International until it was time to rendezvous with Halloran. As he exited the elevator, he suddenly felt the effects of sleep deprivation.

"Ahoy there," shouted Halloran, as Paul entered the lounge. "You're looking a bit faint of form."

"I couldn't nap, but now I feel like I can't stay awake. Would you mind if I pass on dinner and the flick? Sorry I made you come by to pick me up."

"No problem. Better get some rest. You have an eight AM departure for Mwanza, so I'll come by around six-thirty to fetch you."

Paul shook hands with Halloran and returned to his room. He put in a wake-up call and then slipped off his clothes, collapsing on the bed. As he drifted off, he heard laughter from what he figured was the churchyard and the familiar strains of "Pata Pata" by Miriam Makeba, a singer he had discovered in college and loved ever since.

Mama Africa, he thought. *I'm here.*

* * *

His first meeting with the women's group in Mwanza took place in the basement of a nondescript two-story office building on a dirt side street in the center of the city. A dozen females of varying ages greeted him with applause as he entered. Their enthusiasm took him aback, unaccustomed as he was to such an outpouring of delight from his students when he entered a classroom.

"Dr. Stanton, welcome to the Mwanza Women's Cooperative. My name is Akili Zmyuba. Allow me to introduce you to members of our association."

While the young woman formally identified her colleagues, Paul could not keep his eyes off of her. Her silky smooth cocoa complexion, high cheekbones, and voluptuously shaped lips gave her a beauty that set her apart from the other women in her group. Following a morning of his lecturing, Akili escorted him to another room where a table had been set for his lunch.

"This is a typical Tanzanian meal, Dr. Stanton," said Akili. "I hope you like it. Some chai tea, coconut bean soup, and fish ugali, prepared by Mama Kweza, from our class."

"Wonderful. Can you join me?"

"Thank you, but I lunch with the ladies," answered Akili, smiling sweetly, adding, "There is a place to rest over there after you eat, if you desire."

She pointed to a small cot against a far wall, bowed slightly, and left Paul alone to partake of his meal. He found everything quite delicious, if not on the spicy side. While he ate, he could not get the young woman out of his mind. It had been a long time since he was so attracted to someone. Not even his fiancee had inspired such erotic feelings in him. To his bemusement, he found he had an erection just thinking about her.

Whoa, thought Paul, *what's going on here? Keep your head together, old buddy.*

Following the afternoon session, he returned to his hotel. As he sat in the outdoor patio drinking a Kilimanjaro, the local brew, he continued to think about Akili. Somehow she had managed to stir something in him that had long been dormant. Not since college had he experienced such an immediate and passionate attraction to a woman. Now at 56 years old, he did not know what to make of it. While part of him was alarmed by this sudden burst of feelings, another part of him found it exhilarating.

After supper, Paul returned to his room and turned on his portable short wave radio and listened to the BBC World Service news. Unlike in Dar es Salaam, there was no television in his room. Not long into the radio broadcast, he fell asleep. Akili dominated his dreams, and in one she slipped beneath the covers next to him. He awakened expecting her to be there with him and was disappointed when he found she was not.

The next day Paul could hardly focus on his lecture notes as Akili sat in the front row smiling sweetly at him. When the morning session was over, he was again taken to the room where he was given lunch the day before.

"Mama Kweza has prepared duckling and braised cabbage and fruit squash for you, Dr. Stanton," said Akili, placing the dishes on the table.

"Please call me Paul."

"Yes...Dr. *Paul*," replied Akili, looking at him intensely, her tongue moving slowly across her bottom lip.

An uncontrollable urge overtook Paul, and he drew her into his arms and kissed her hard. To his great satisfaction and relief, she reciprocated. In the next instant they were making love on the sagging bed. Paul could not recall ever having such an intense sexual encounter. Akili's fingers explored every part of his body as he pushed into her as far as he could reach. When they had expended themselves, they lay drenched in perspiration on the narrow mattress, their hearts pounding against one another's heated flesh. Their reverie was suddenly broken when a member of the women's cooperative entered the room, calling out for Akili. As soon as she saw their naked bodies, she froze, her eyes bulging from their sockets.

"Akili? *Pardon . . . please*," she sputtered and ran from the room.

Akili giggled, surprising Paul, who expected her to be mortified.

"It is okay, Dr. Paul," she assured him, putting on her brightly colored khanga. "Do not worry."

But Paul was worried. *It was inappropriate and unseemly to behave in such a manner*, he thought, pulling up his pants. When he returned to the classroom, he found everyone awaiting him, including the woman who had caught him and Akili in a compromised state. She averted her eyes when he looked at her, but Akili smiled at him knowingly, reigniting his passion. It took several moments for him to gather his thoughts enough to deliver his afternoon lecture. By the end the day, he felt he had masked his turbulent emotions enough to do what was required of him. However, it was anything but a stellar lecture, he conceded to himself.

"Thank you Dr. Paul . . . ah, *Stanton*," said Akili, leading her cohorts in applause.

That evening as he mulled over his indiscretion with Akili, there was a knock on his hotel door. Believing it was Akili, Paul dashed to open it. Before him was a tall young man, whose piercing black eyes appeared like burning coals.

"You be Dr. Stanton?" he asked in broken English.

"Yes, that's me. What can I do for you?"

"You have violated my woman, Miss Akili," he replied, his expression hardening.

"Who are you, and why do you say that?" replied Paul, his heart rate surging.

"I am Shaka. I am told you seduced my woman, who I am to marry."

Paul closed the door slightly to keep the stranger from reaching him should he launch an attack.

"I don't know what you're talking about, and I did not know Akili was engaged."

"She is no longer respectable to have as wife. So I end my future with her."

"Wait," said Paul, but the man continued to speak.

"For your evil deed, I place a curse on you. You will be sorry for what you did," shouted the aggrieved stranger, heaving a red powdery substance at him and dashing away.

"Hey!" yelped Paul, brushing the strange dust from his body.

What the hell have I got myself into? he wondered, resolving to avoid all intimate contact with Akili for the remaining week he had in Tanzania. But as soon as he saw her in class, his determination was shaken, and all he could think about was renewing his affair with her. By the day of his departure, he and Akili had become as one, and the fire of their passion had repeatedly reached powerful new heights.

"Will you come back, Dr. Paul?" asked Akili, abjectly.

"If I can, but I will write to you," promised Paul, climbing into the cab that would take him to his Air Tanzania flight back to Dar es Salaam and a connection to the States.

"I know you will return to me . . . I *know*. I love you, Dr. Paul," shouted Akili, as the cab pulled away.

Paul wondered if he loved her as well, but he was certain she had taken a piece of his heart. Still, he was relieved to be returning stateside and thankful that Akili's former beau had not confronted him again. On the long trip home, Akili filled his thoughts, and he began to suspect she would remain there for a very long time.

* * *

Paul's fiancee, Mary Billings, was eagerly awaiting his arrival at Boston's Logan Airport. He was besieged by guilt as soon as he caught sight of her small figure at the end of the long concourse. *You idiot! Now what?* he pondered, and at that moment decided to keep his African liaison secret. However, it had never been in his nature to be deceitful, and as soon as he embraced Mary, he felt despicable. Nonetheless, he pretended he was delighted to see his longtime girlfriend, but the fact was Akili had taken the whole of his affection. Paul felt only sadness that Mary would soon realize their life together was over. He planned to wait things out before admitting he could not marry her, but he resolved never to tell her why. He wondered if his feelings would change over time, but doubted they would.

Very quickly, of course, Mary had sensed and then realized things had changed between her and Paul. Most of the time they were together he seemed unusually quiet, even sullen. It was all too clear to her that his thoughts were elsewhere. Eventually, she confronted him about his behavior, and he contrived an answer that only added to her uncertainty and frustration.

"I'm so sorry. Something has happened to me. I just don't want to get married. I thought I did, but now it doesn't make sense to me. Marriage is such a . . .."

"Doesn't make sense to you? I don't understand," protested Mary. "You were the one who proposed. Now it doesn't make sense to you. Well, *that* doesn't make sense to me."

Mary removed her engagement ring and handed it to Paul. Wiping tears from her eyes, she rose and left the restaurant where they had met. They had planned to attend a Canter College Music Ensemble performance after supper. The very next day, Paul experienced an uncontrollable explosion of flatulence while lecturing to his Introduction of Finance class. He was mortified, although his students could not conceal their amusement. Loud hiccups forced him to dismiss his next class.

Jesus, he thought, *what the hell did I eat?* His bizarre physical manifestations disappeared as soon as he left campus, only to return during his next round of classes two days later. Not only were the gas and hiccups back in full force, but now he could not keep from stuttering. Paul made an appointment with his doctor, who ordered a round of tests. The results were negative, although the symptoms resurfaced every time he attempted to teach. Forlorn, Paul began to cancel classes, and soon he put in for a medical leave.

Why is this happening? he fretted, and then out of the blue an improbable explanation occurred to him. *The curse . . . it's Shaka's curse.* Although Akili continued to dominate his thoughts, he had resisted communicating with her.

Now he wrote her a letter explaining in detail what was happening to him. But before he received a reply, he decided to return to Mwanza and confront Akili's distraught former beau. He also desperately longed to see Akili again.

When he landed in Mwanza, he was shocked to see Akili waiting for him at the dilapidated airport.

"How did you know I'd be back?" he asked, wrapping his arms around her.

"I have come here every day since you left because I knew you would return to me."

"You knew?" inquired Paul, looking lovingly into the face that had been emblazoned on his mind.

"Yes, I placed Yoruba on you."

"A what?"

"A spell that returns lost lovers."

"So it wasn't Shaka?" asked Paul, bewildered.

"Of course, not. He is silly man. I am heir to the wizard *Mohana*. I placed a spell on him to leave... and another on you to return, and it has come to pass," revealed Akili, her dark face beaming radiantly.

It took a moment for Akili's admission to register in Paul's mind. When it did, he realized he had been totally bewitched by the beautiful Tanzanian sorceress from the instant he set eyes on her.

Gabriel's Response to a Casual Inquiry

You've used up all your heaven.

Life has given you all it has.

Only those short-changed,

get a death bonus.

Take the Second Left on Your Right

He is lost to the forest.
—Sir Walter Scott

Navigating the narrow, one-way streets of downtown Boston required a host of virtues, foremost among them patience. It was not a personality trait Emil Clayton possessed. This was never more evident than when he was behind the wheel in heavy traffic or, even worse, when he was lost. He would quickly lose it and curse everything in his path, especially drivers who were elderly or female—or both. His wife, Carla, had experienced his outrages countless times and dreaded them. He was impossible to placate in this frenzied state. Carla would try her best to tune him out, but she was seldom able to do so.

On numerous occasions she had made clear her displeasure with his over-the-top behavior, but it only intensified his ire, resulting in a nasty shouting match and a prolonged period of icy silence when all was said and done. The experience was all too familiar, and Carla had finally reached the end of her tether.

"No more! I can't take you going ballistic like this. It's scary. You really have some anger issues."

"Only when I have to deal with idiot drivers and the medieval streets in this frigging city," protested Emil.

"Get over it. You've been like this since we got married. You'll have a heart attack. You should see yourself. Your face is contorted and veins pop out of your temples. You look psycho. Doctor Jekyll and Mr. Hyde," replied Carla, disgustedly.

Stung by her comments, Emil began to calm down. "I know. I'm sorry. I just lose it," he said contritely.

His meltdown was always followed by a period of remorse and self-loathing.

"No kidding. I'm so tired of it. You say this after every explosion, and then it happens again and again."

Emil had little to offer in his defense. He had to agree that in his driving behavior, he was a jerk—there was no getting around it. As usual, he sank into a dark funk over his indefensible behavior. No further words were exchanged until his hangdog expression would diffuse his wife's displeasure.

"I think you have to remind yourself about how crazy you become when you're in traffic or lost. Maybe you should get one of those GPS things," Carla offered.

"I don't know," replied Emil grimly.

"My brother loves his."

"Your brother is a gadget freak. He buys anything new."

"GPS devices are hardly new. Many drivers use them. You really need to get one, so you don't stroke out."

"I'll think about it," muttered Emil.

"Get one. I can't put up with this any longer. If you don't, I'm not riding with you into town any more."

"I'll see," replied Emil, as he parked the car next to the restaurant where they had reservations.

"What do you know, we're ten minutes early after all your freaking out about being late," observed Carla.

Embarrassed, Emil attempted to redirect his wife's justifiable harangue, but he failed and they shared few words over dinner. The ride home was no more animated. *Shit, this frost will last for a while. I better look for a used GPS on eBay,* thought Emil. If he could get one cheap, he would buy it to get back in the good graces of his wife. The idea of actually using it did not really interest him.

* * *

Emil finally did go online to find a previously owned GPS. For $50, he purchased a "like new" Tom-Tom. But true to form, it remained in its package until Carla pressed him to put it in his vehicle.

"For heaven's sake, try it out. You might actually like it," grumbled Carla, while her husband held it gingerly like he would have a dirty diaper. "We can use it on our trip."

It was just two days before they were to travel to upstate New York to pick up a Golden Retriever puppy from a breeder—a replacement for their longtime beloved dog that had died a few weeks earlier. The day before they were set to go, however, Carla twisted her knee and could barely walk, so it was left to Emil to fetch their new pet.

"Make sure you use the GPS. By the time you get back, you'll be an expert with it," said Carla, applying an ice pack to her injury.

Emil had read up on the device and actually found himself somewhat intrigued with it.

"It *is* a pretty neat thing," admitted Emil, to his wife's considerable satisfaction.

"Well, listen to you, Mr. Luddite," she responded with an approving smile.

"I'll see if it really knows the way," said Emil, readying himself for what he estimated to be a four to five hour drive.

"Be careful," said Carla, lying on the couch with her afflicted leg elevated, as Emil blew her a kiss.

"You be careful, too. Watch that knee. I'll be back tonight with the puppy," answered Emil.

He had programmed the GPS according to the manual, but forgot to turn it on until he was on Route 95.

Take a right onto the Mass Pike ahead two-thirds of a mile, instructed a pleasant female voice from the dashboard-mounted instrument.

"Will do, sweetie," replied Emil. "Hope you know where we're going. You chicks aren't famous for your sense of direction. Maybe you got a guy there to help you?" he asked, half-jokingly—allowing a second to pass before answering his own question. "No? Well, I guess I'm at your mercy, so lead the way."

* * *

The voice on the GPS had sounded faintly familiar to Emil from the moment he heard it, and halfway to his destination, he realized why. It possessed the vocal qualities—or more succinctly the lack of any distinctive voice qualities––of a college girlfriend he had jilted long ago. After five months of what had become a tempestuous relationship with the computer programming major, Emil had met another woman who would become his future wife. When he informed his girlfriend that he was ending their rocky union, she threw a tantrum and tossed a wine glass at him. It had narrowly missed his face. Yet her outbursts didn't end there. Three days later she accosted him at the student union, intent upon heaving a cup of hot coffee at him. Fortunately she dropped the steaming brew before she could launch it at him.

For two months, she stalked him, but only once had she made actual contact with him. It was to ask if they could hook up again for one last date. "Just a farewell fuck," was how she had put it. Emil explained that he was now in a committed relationship, and she responded by telling him that it would never be over between them—that someday he would be hers again. After that he spotted her a couple of more times—once spying on him from behind a tree and another time walking across the snow-covered campus in his direction. He had retreated into a dorm to avoid her.

A year passed and then he heard that she had dropped out of school. He was relieved by the news but wondered if he had been the cause of her departure. As time passed, however, she finally faded from his thoughts. Until now, that is.

Turn right at exit 41, directed the GPS.

"Hey, Sabrina . . . Sabby. Long time no hear . . . fortunately. How've you been all these years?"

Continue for eighteen miles . . ..

"Ever find happiness? I mean, find someone who could put up with you. You were pretty daft, so if you did, he probably dumped you, too."

Emil continued talking to the GPS. It entertained him and made the time pass quickly. It was also nice to vent at an approximation of someone who had briefly made his life a misery.

"Think you were the type that would find some poor unsuspecting jerk to get you pregnant so he'd be forced to marry you. Then you'd murder your family while they slept."

Take the second left on your right, advised the Sabrina-like voice on the GPS.

"Huh?" muttered Emil, confused.

Take the second left after the next right.

"Oh, that makes more sense. Guess I heard you wrong," said Emil, in mock regret.

He followed the directions but was perplexed when the second left turned out to be a dead end. He reset the GPS, and it instructed him to drive north to Route 31 west.

"I'm losing my patience with you, but we've been there before . . . haven't we, Sabby?" remarked Emil, as he drove out of the *cul de sac*.

* * *

As Emil cruised along Route 3 toward Gouveneur and the puppy that awaited him, he was caught up in the beauty of the Adirondack Mountains that surrounded him. It was a place he had spent part of a summer with his parents as a child, and he was glad to return. The GPS voice broke his reverie.

Take Route 56 north one mile.

"Right oh, Sabby. Your wish is my command," replied Emil.

When the time came to change roads Emil was surprised to find himself on a single lane black top without a centerline.

"Hope you're right about this, old gal," said Emil, as he sped down the desolate strip of asphalt edged on both sides by encroaching woods.

Half an hour later Emil became concerned by the total absence of any human presence.

Take the next left at McComber Road, directed the GPS.

In less than a mile, he reached the turn, which consisted of little more than a gravel path just wide enough for a car.

"Whoa, Sabby. This can't be right. Where the hell you taking me?"

Emil pulled over and fished a map from the glove compartment.

"No offense, but I'm going to check a more reliable source . . . Mr. Rand McNally," said Emil, unfolding the New England road guide. "There's Route 56 . . . Crap, the damn map only shows a piece of it," grumbled Emil. "Should have brought along a New York State atlas."

Continue ahead for three miles to Route . . . .

Several moments of silence followed.

"Yeah? To Route what?" blurted Emil, his frustration mounting.

No answer came, and when he tried to reset the GPS, its function was unresponsive.

Great! No GPS and no map. I'm screwed, thought Emil, who then decided to drive on hoping he would reach the unidentified route.

He drove well past the three miles the GPS had indicated, and then he considered turning around. The road was so narrow and the brush so thick on either side of it that he could find no place to attempt a round about. He had no choice but to follow the road wherever it led, and Emil began to wonder if it led anywhere.

"Take the second left on your right," instructed the Sabby-like voice of the digital navigator.

"Not that shit again, you crazy bitch!" snapped Emil, tightening his grip on the steering wheel.

Then the road divided.

Take the second left on your right, repeated the GPS.

"What the . . . ? Okay, I'll stay right and look for a second left," he muttered, desperately.

Sure enough there appeared a second road to the left, and it was only a few yards beyond the first turn. By now the sun had set, forcing Emil to follow the beams of his headlights.

Continue ahead, instructed the GPS over and over as Emil's apprehension grew exponentially.

Again, he considered turning back, but there was no doing so. The road was even narrower than the one he left a few miles back. Tree limbs reached from the sides and scrabbled against his car. Emil feared the road would eventually constrict like a clogged artery, making it impossible to move forward.

Back up. Get the hell out of here, he thought, but when he put the car in reverse, he found he had no back up lights.

"Jesus," he whined. "This can't be happening."

Continue ahead, directed the GPS, and Emil hit the off switch.

"You douchebag!!" he bellowed.

Continue ahead . . . continue ahead, repeated the GPS, despite having its power cut.

Get out and walk back to the main road, Emil told himself.

To his horror, he found the doors of his car held tightly closed by the impenetrable wall of trees.

"No," he whimpered, and pressed the accelerator.

"The car would not move in reverse, so he jammed it into drive and it lurched forward. For another twenty minutes, Emil drove in the only direction he could while the GPS urged him on.

"What the hell is going on?" repeated Emil, on the verge of sobbing.

His dread was compounded when the gas gauge warning light came on.

"I'm trapped! I'm fucking trapped!" he howled, and then he spotted a light in the distance. "Oh, thank God!"

He pressed the gas pedal as far as it would go not caring that it caused the tree limbs to bump against his car. He could not have cared less if the car was damaged beyond repair as long as he could get out of his untenable situation. All he wanted was to reach civilization and end his nightmare.

As he approached the lighted structure, the GPS declared that he had reached his destination. Before him in a small clearing was a pristine dwelling adorned in flower boxes. It reminded Emil of the cottage in *Hansel and Gretel*.

Is this the kennel? Emil wondered. He stopped the car and surveyed the area. There were no fences or signs of a dog run. The perfectly groomed landscape suggested it was an unlikely place for dogs to be raised and trained. It did not resemble any kennel he had seen.

You have reached the end of the road, declared the GPS.

"The end of the road is right," Emil mumbled, deciding to inquire within about his location and get directions that would not take him back over the roads he'd just traveled. *I'll never go back that way*, he promised himself . . . *never*.

He climbed the steps of the porch that led to the front door and rang the bell. In the distance he heard the chimes sound the first few notes of Bach's "Abide With Me." The door slowly opened, and before him stood the last person he ever wanted to see again.

"I knew you'd find your way back to me," said Sabrina, her arms outstretched in greeting.

Only she could hear Emil's anguished cry . . . and that pleased her.

Road Kill

To err is human, not to, animal.
—Robert Frost

As Afra emerged from the woods, she encountered strange shimmering objects roaring past her. Not knowing what they were, she stepped into the clearing intent on reaching the pine trees on the other side. The peculiar moving forms confused and frightened her, but she forged ahead in quest of her missing fawn, Dympna. A few feet into the treeless area, she was struck with such force that she became airborne, eventually landing on the hard surface. Everything went black for a moment and then she regained consciousness. Her body was racked with pain the likes of which she'd never known—pain far beyond what she had experienced falling into a frozen pond or being grazed by a hunter's bullet. The awful hurt was centered mainly in her right leg, which was snapped in half and resting inches from her bleeding nose.

While Afra lay gravely injured, she noticed that the passing objects contained what she knew as slayers of her breed. Some stared at her with mild curiosity while others ignored her entirely, continuing on their way. When she attempted to right herself, agony immobilized her. A second attempt to stand resulted in a shift in her position on the road and a near collision with another vehicle.

The wounded doe remained unassisted as the sun began to descend the western sky. She could feel her heartbeat slow and the pain ebb, as her body grew numb. She no longer felt the harsh blasts of wind generated by the migrating vessels containing the enemies of her species.

My child . . . my dear child, she moaned, fearing she would never see her only offspring again.

Was the father of her fawn nearby, she wondered? He, too, had been searching for their lost youngster.

Maral . . . Maral! Called Afra, but she lacked the strength to be heard beyond the immediate vicinity. Nonetheless, she continued her desperate summons. More than anything, she hoped the herd's lead buck would find Dympna and escape with her into the deep forest where they would be beyond the deadly acts of humans.

From the corner of her eye, she saw a vessel stop and two humans climb out and walk in her direction. Hoping to ward them off, she tried to swing her head in a threatening manner, but her movement was slight and did not deter them.

"She got some life in her yet, but not much," said one of the humans.

"Some nice meat there. She's a pretty full cow . . . way too big to get in the car whole like that," observed his companion.

"We can drag her to the shoulder and cut her up there. Take the good stuff. Got my machete and a tarp in the trunk we can wrap it in."

"Better put her down before moving her. These things can be dangerous in that condition. Can kick you dead."

"No biggie. Just slit her jugular and she's a goner."

A vehicle with flashing yellow lights pulled up behind Afra and the men.

"Damn! It's the highway guys come to clear her off. They gonna' want her steaks. Divide her up in the truck. Maybe sell the meat."

As the men discussed the situation, Afra fought to remain conscious. At one point, a passing auto came to a near stop. For a split second, Afra made eye contact with a child sitting in the back seat. The small human's guileless brown eyes reminded her of Dympna, prompting a mournful whine to burst forth from her damaged lungs. The hunters stepped back and were almost glanced by a van.

"Shoot, she ain't that far gone!" observed one of them, as the highway officials approached.

"You boys best get off the road before you end up like this poor critter. We'll take care of things from here," said a tall figure in a bright orange vest.

"Okay, man. We're gone," replied one of the hunters.

"Yeah, enjoy the meat, fellas," said the other, with a snide tone in his voice.

The banished men reluctantly climbed into their pickup and drove off, scattering gravel with its spinning tires.

" Fools!" spit one of the highway officials, shaking his fist.

"Never mind them. Back the truck up a little more, Sid, so we can hoist her carcass onto the flatbed. I'll dart her," instructed the other road worker, aiming a pistol at the wounded deer and firing it.

Afra did not feel the dart strike her neck, but within seconds she could no longer hold up her head. As her world was about to go dark, she caught a glimpse of her precious fawn emerging from the dense brush. Terrified for its welfare, Afra willed herself to find the strength to warn Dympna against entering the hazardous clearance. Her admonition did not work, because the young animal wanted nothing more than to reach her mother.

The screech of tires and a horrible thud were the last things Afra ever heard.

Redemption Lake

*Far darker and far more terrible
will be the day of their return.*
—Lord Macaulay

Daryl Spooner watched in dismay as the small plane wavered in the air, then flipped over, and plunged toward the lake. Before he could catch its image on his cellphone, it hit the water with a thunderous splash, causing debris to fly in all directions. As quickly as he could, he drove his outboard boat toward the mishap to try to rescue the survivors. There would be survivors, Daryl thought with certainty, approaching the crash site. Thus it was no surprise to him when two figures emerged from the lake, choking and waving frantically for help.

Daryl lifted the stunned man and woman into his boat. Neither was hurt and their clothes were even dry. He wasn't surprised, as he had seen this before– the first time when his six-year old daughter had fallen from the pier while chasing a ball. Although the water was not deep at that point, the submerged rocks would have been—should have been—lethal. But she was fine, only a bit shaken by the experience. Daryl had fetched her from the water moments after she fell, and he was relieved and astounded to find her uninjured and barely wet.

On another occasion, Daryl had witnessed a collision between two speeding

Skidoos driven by teenagers. The crash had sent both youths airborne, as their crafts slumped to a halt. Again, Daryl had jumped into his outboard and raced to the aid of the accident victims only to find them totally unscathed and even recounting the incident to each other with great amusement. Alcohol was clearly a factor in their wreck, concluded Daryl, who fished the carefree survivors from the water.

That contretemps had occurred last summer on the very day he and his family were to return home after a week at the lake. Now, on this, the last day of their vacation, Daryl had fished yet another pair of mis-adventurers from the water in what should have been a fatal outcome.

Daryl swung his aluminum skiff around and headed to shore as the couple he had just plucked from the lake clutched one another, the woman sobbing softly.

"Jesus, we're hardly wet! How can that be?" asked the man, incredulously.

"What happened up there?" inquired Daryl, nodding skyward.

"The engine caught fire. Then we just went into a spin," responded the man, who introduced himself and his wife.

"Good to meet you . . . *Marv and Gale*," replied Daryl. "Where you folks from?"

"Traverse City. On our way to Toronto," answered the husband, checking his cellphone. "No service out here, huh?"

"Got a landline in my cabin. Better call 911 when we get there," replied Daryl, navigating his boat to the small dock at the edge of his property.

* * *

The Spooners were forced to delay their trip home due to the long round of questions by the authorities about the plane crash. Their ride home was further forestalled due to an overturned truck less than a mile from their cabin.

"What's T-O-X-I-C spell, daddy?" asked young Laurie Spooner, gazing out of the car window.

"It spells *toxic*, honey," replied Daryl.

"What's that mean?"

"It means . . . ah, poison. Something bad for you, darling," replied her father, tentatively.

"Does it hurt?"

"Yes, if you touch or eat it. But it won't bother us here, Laurie."

"It's a Kramer Chemical truck from the nearby plant," observed Nicki Spooner, to her husband.

"Carrying hydrofluoric acid. Stuff is nasty," added Daryl.

The Spooners were kept from passing the scene for over an hour. During that time, Daryl learned that the tanker had been split open, resulting in a massive spill.

"Trooper says it will contaminate everything for miles," reported Daryl, shaking his head in disgust.

"Might take away the powers of your magical lake," said Nicki, in a smug tone.

"Ha!! You'd like that, I bet," snapped Daryl.

"Honey, I just think you get carried away by all this. Strange things happen and people don't always die."

"And what about Laurie? Was that just a coincidence?" challenged Daryl.

"God was watching out for her."

"Now that's an interesting theory. God chose to save our daughter and let a million kids in Africa die of starvation."

"Makes more sense than a lake that brings people back to life, don't you think?"

"Maybe," conceded Daryl, adding, "but I think surviving a plane that crashes into the lake is pretty damn unusual."

"It is, honey, but people come through all sorts of weird accidents."

"Five people came out of that lake alive when they should have died. That seems more than a series of *weird* accidents," retorted Daryl.

"Keep your eyes on the road, or we'll have a not-so-weird accident," countered Nicki, as the Spooners' car entered the interstate on the last leg of their journey back to Ann Arbor.

* * *

Two days after Christmas the Spooners returned to their northern Michigan cabin for their customary week of cross-country skiing and ice skating. Thus far the amount of snowfall had been negligible in Ann Arbor, and reports indicated conditions were the same up at the lake.

"At least it's been pretty cold. We'll be able to get plenty of skating in," said Daryl, in response to his wife's belief that they should have held off until there was snow.

"We could have taken you-know-who to you-know-where," replied Laurie, making reference to their longtime plan to go to Disney World with their daughter.

"It's a mob scene down there this time of year, besides we'll probably get snow while we're up here. We always do."

As they approached the turn to the gravel road leading to their cabin, they noticed a long stretch of yellow hazard tape blocking the woods on their right.

"The tanker spill, I guess," observed Daryl.

"Hope it didn't contaminate our property," commented Nicki, warily.

"Well, there's no tape on this side of the road. Maybe they got most of it cleaned up," replied Daryl, pulling up to the cabin.

"Yippee!" shouted Laurie, leaping from the car. "Let's go skating."

"Looks good," observed Daryl, scanning the lake. "Nice and frozen. Let's get our stuff in the house, and then we'll head out."

"Not me," responded Nicki. "I'm going to make a nice fire and read my book."

"Suit yourself, honey."

"Yeah, *honey*," mimicked Laurie, causing her parents to chuckle.

"You guys go ahead. I'll unload this stuff," offered Nicki.

"Yeah, come on, daddy. Let's go."

Father and daughter grabbed their skates and dashed to the lake's edge, where they quickly put them on.

"Be careful," yelled Nicki, lugging a box of groceries to the cabin.

"Always," answered Daryl, as he and Laurie moved onto the ice.

"Always," echoed Laurie, letting go of her father's hand.

* * *

The wind swept across the open lake and made Daryl shiver, although he felt exhilarated by the purity and sereneness of the surroundings.

"Pull your hat down over your ears, honey," shouted Daryl to his daughter, who had moved ahead of him.

It was evident to Daryl that his daughter was a natural on the ice. She glided gracefully across the frozen lake showing no hesitation from the year off the blades. That was not true for Daryl, who moved tentatively in her direction.

"Don't go too far, honey," called Daryl, as his daughter sped away.

A strange scent filled Daryl's nostrils. It was not altogether disagreeable, but it was foreign to him, and when he looked closely at the ice, he thought it appeared slightly discolored, pinkish. When he returned his gaze to his daughter, she was gone, and his heart jumped. He quickly scanned the lake's expanse and shouted her name. Racing to where he had last seen her, he saw a break in the ice. He knew she had gone under, and he panicked. Just as he was about to leap in after her, he spotted her hat and grabbed for it. It was still on her head, as Daryl tugged at it.

"Daddy, I fell in," she said, calmly, and Daryl knew the lake had saved her as it had the others.

"I know, sweetheart, but you'll be okay," said Daryl, lifting her from the frigid water.

Against her protests, he skated back to the cabin with her in his arms.

"I want to skate some more," she said, twisting her body in an attempt to free herself from her father's tight embrace.

"Later, honey. I think we need to get to the cabin and warm you up," Daryl replied.

"Why? I'm not cold."

She was right, observed Daryl. Her skin was warm and her clothes were dry.

"Just for a while, and then we'll come back out," promised Daryl, wondering if he should say anything about the latest extraordinary incident to his skeptical wife.

Since returning home last summer, Nicki had made him swear to say nothing further about what she called his "lake fantasy," and he had kept his promise in order to keep the peace.

"For the love of God, Daryl, please stop talking about this nonsense to everyone. They think you're losing it. It's embarrassing," she had lamented, after a gathering in which he had recounted his lake experiences.

"Could be aliens in the lake," his neighbor had joked, prompting every one at the barbecue to laugh.

* * *

By the time Daryl had returned to the cabin with his daughter, he had decided to throw caution to the wind and tell his wife what happened. Laurie would corroborate his account, and maybe that would convince Nicki that, indeed, something miraculous was going on in the lake.

"Why are you carrying her, Daryl?" asked Nicki, as he entered the house. "Is something the matter?"

"She went through the ice," explained Daryl.

"Oh, my God!" shrieked Nicki, running to where they stood. "Are you okay, sweetheart? How did that happen? Weren't you with her, Daryl?"

"Mommy, it was fun," said Laurie, reaching for her mother.

"She skated ahead and then she went through the ice. I don't know how, because it's thick where she entered," explained Daryl. "But I reached in and got her, and she was okay . . . like the people on the plane and the kids on the Skiddo."

"She's dry. What the . . .?"

"Yeah, just like they were. I told you that," replied Daryl.

"Did you really fall into the ice, honey?" asked Nicki, skeptically.

"I want to go skating, mommy," replied Laurie, ignoring her question and moving to the door.

"Answer mommy, honey," implored Daryl.

"Can I go . . . *please*?" asked his daughter, opening the door.

"I can't believe this. You made this whole thing up to get me to believe your crazy stories," growled Nicki, going to Laurie, who was halfway out the door.

"What are you saying? I would never make up such a tale. That's ridiculous!" protested Daryl, as his wife and daughter exited the cabin.

They returned a couple of hours later, having hiked through the woods, and Daryl greeted them as they climbed the steps to the porch.

"Look at the sunset. It's amazing," said Daryl, pointing across the lake.

The early evening sky was a brilliant red, causing the frozen body of water to give off a shimmering crimson glow.

"I've never seen it like that. It's gorgeous. Like a painting," commented his wife, transfixed by the otherworldly scene before her.

"Mommy, I'm hot," complained Laurie, whose skin appeared flushed.

"Maybe she's catching cold from her *fall* through the ice," said Nicki, smirking at her husband.

"Yeah, maybe she is," replied Daryl, defensively.

* * *

The Spooners spent the evening reading stories to their daughter from her favorite books, and when she went to bed, they sat silently before the fire until they, too, turned in. Their sleep was disrupted by their daughter's cries, which quickly took them to her room. When Nicki turned on the lamp next to her daughter's bed, she let out a loud shriek. Her daughter's arms and neck were covered with what appeared to be scales.

"Daryl! Daryl!" screamed Nicki, backing away from her daughter, who suddenly rose from the bed, revealing claw-like hands and feet.

Laurie then leapt toward her shocked parents, swinging at them violently. A deep guttural noise emanated from her throat, which sounded like the word "run." Daryl and his wife dashed from the cabin, their monstrously transformed daughter in close pursuit. The Spooners soon found themselves on the frozen lake with their path blocked by their crazed child.

"Oh, my God! Laurie . . . *Laurie*! What's happened to you?" cried Nicki.

At that point, the ice broke under them. As they sank into the freezing lake, they heard laughter and the barely discernable chant, "Rise up, mother and father . . . rise up."

In an instant they were lifted from the water onto the ice that covered it. They were no longer terrified. In fact, a feeling of calmness overtook them. Near them stood their daughter appearing like the child they adored.

"See," said Daryl, breathlessly. "The lake changes everything."

"Are you okay, Laurie?" asked Nicki, clutching at her dry clothing puzzled.

"I'm fine, mommy. Why?"

"There *is* something going on . . . some kind of strange power here," conceded Nicki to her husband, wrapping her arms around him and their restored daughter as they carefully skated across the ice.

"Yes . . . yes, I know there is," he answered, grateful for her long-withheld acknowledgment.

* * *

The Spooners returned to their cabin and lit the fireplace, but it felt too warm to them, and they went to the porch to cool off, stripping away their winter gear. As the hours passed, their flesh began to scale over. When they saw this happen to each other, it pleased rather than horrified them.

"Look, daddy," said Laurie, pointing to the cabin just south of theirs on the shoreline.

The family owning it had arrived for their usual winter break.

"Can we stay another day and go skating with them?" she pleaded, with a sweetness that they could never resist.

"What do you think, Mother? Another day on the lake can't hurt, right?"

Daryl asked his smiling wife.

"Oh, I don't think it would hurt at all," responded Nicki, and the Spooner family squealed with delight as they flexed their razor-sharp talons.

Baby Love

*A direful death indeed they had
That would put any parent mad.*
—Marjory Fleming

The Morgans' happiest day was when their son, Joshua, was born. Their darkest day came only a month later.

"I'm afraid there's a problem. Your son's scan shows poor amygdala function," reported Dr. Logan, a neurologist at the Infant Neuroscience Institute.

"And that means?" asked Chris Morgan, hesitantly.

"Well, it's indicative of likely psychopathic behavior in adulthood."

"Oh God!" blurted Fran Morgan, "What can we do? Is there a way of stopping this?"

"Nothing that we know about at the present time. Compounding the situation is your son's lower than normal volume of orbital frontal cortex, which regulates sociability. Now that may change over time through general physical maturation. That is, as he gets older it may catch up to the size it should be. But that is not the case with the limbic system, of which the amygdala is a part. It doesn't conform to human growth patterns.

"What happens as they get older?" inquired Chris.

"Children with this syndrome often exhibit what psychologists call 'callous-unemotional traits.' They don't feel guilt or emotions about wrongdoings. They lack sympathy for the pain of others. Not infrequently, witnessing others' suffering may be fascinating, even quite pleasurable. There can be other conduct problems as well. That is why they're dispatched the first year."

"We shouldn't have had this test done," whimpered Fran, sobbing softly.

"Mrs. Morgan, you know the law requires that all new infants be tested," responded Dr. Logan. "It guarantees a safer, better future for everyone.

"We don't have a choice," replied Chris, patting his wife's knee.

"Poor little Joshua. It's not fair," gasped Fran, wiping her cheek.

"So what happens next, doctor? Isn't there something . . .?" asked Chris, beginning to tear up.

"Regrettably, there are no options. The infant must be euthanized by his first birthday according to regulations. This gives you time with your child, if you like. However, many parents prefer to act right away before they get too attached and bond with their offspring. Believe me, this will be better for everyone concerned. The world doesn't need another serial killer."

"Serial killer!! How can you say that about an innocent baby?" snapped Fran, leaping from her chair.

"I'm sorry for being so blunt about this, Mrs. Morgan. I know it's terribly painful, but research predicts that over 90 percent of children with your son's defect will become homicidal. That's why the government requires termination once such a diagnosis is made. It is in the best interest of society."

"Never!" shouted Fran. "I will not have my child murdered."

"There is a positive side to this, Mrs. Morgan, if you choose to look at it that way. His organs will be harvested to benefit those babies with non-neurological deficiencies . . . babies that are repairable," offered Logan.

"You're the murderers here. Not the poor helpless children you condemn to death."

"Please, honey. Calm down," appealed Chris.

"It's our baby we're talking about here. You want him to die because of some test?"

"No . . . *no*," spluttered her flustered husband.

"How do you know you're right about this, doctor?" inquired Fran, staring harshly at the neurologist.

"We'll be happy to repeat the scans, but I'm confident the results will be the same."

"You people are so smug. What if it was your baby? Would you be so quick to condemn him?"

"The Institute just provides the testing, Mrs. Morgan. We don't moralize, although we believe in its purpose."

"Thanks for nothing," growled Fran, stomping from the office.

"Sorry, doc," said her husband, following in her footsteps.

* * *

That night the Morgans sat by the crib of their sleeping child and wept.

"Look at him. He's like an angel. How can he grow up to become a criminal? I think they don't know what they're doing," said Fran, her head against her husband's shoulder.

"The INI doctors are the foremost experts on genetics and neuroscience in the country. They discovered the process for determining these things," replied Chris Morgan.

"And look what's come of it. Babies are being killed," said Fran, stiffening.

"I'm as devastated by this as you are. I hate that we found this out, but I can't deny the facts."

"What? That our baby is a future monster?"

"You know that's not what I'm saying," countered Chris, defensively.

"So we should have him put down like a rabid dog? Well, I won't allow it!" screamed Fran, causing the baby to wake and cry. "There . . . there, sweetheart," whispered Fran, cradling the child in her arms.

"I would never let them kill our baby," responded Chris, defensively. "We'll do something before the time comes . . .."

"We can move away," offered Fran, hopefully.

"You know that's impossible. They'd just track the chips," said Chris, pointing to the back of his neck.

"We can remove them. Others have done that."

"But not successfully . . . as we both know."

"We should try, Chris. After all, we'd be doing it for Joshua."

"What about the INI results?" countered Chris.

"Oh, that's right," replied Fran, sarcastically. "Our baby is defective, and he's going to start murdering people before he's in kindergarten."

"Then we have to come up with a plan."

"What kind of plan?"

"Fake his death. Say we threw him in the bay. Wanted to do it our way, and so on."

"And then what? They'll search for Joshua. How can we hide him?"

"We can't keep him, but we don't have to let them kill him. We'll find an adoption center and give him to a couple looking for a child."

"But what about those damning test results? No one will want him."

"I can forge a state certificate stating he's healthy. At least then he'll have a chance."

"My poor little baby," said Fran forlornly, returning Joshua to his crib.

* * *

It took the Morgans two months to implement their plan to spare their son's life. During that time, they Googled dozens of adoption agencies located hundreds of miles away from their home, finally settling on one in Des Moines, Iowa. The computer images of the parenting service appealed to them and they believed its distance from their home in D.C. would keep the authorities from finding Joshua, who had not been fitted with a locator.

"Well, it looks like a reputable place," observed Fran, her nose inches from the computer monitor.

"Nobody will be looking for us, because we haven't violated any law. We'll just drive there. Pay cash for everything. No paper trail. Joshua will simply vanish. They'll never find him way out there," said Chris, reassuringly.

Their plan involved staking out the mid-western adoption agency in the early morning hours before it opened and leaving the baby at its entrance. They would affix the fake certificate to his garment showing their child had satisfactorily passed the neurological screening for defects.

"He'll have a life and a chance this way," said Chris, attempting to placate his wife's reluctance, as they sat in their car across from the adoption office.

"Not yet . . . please," pleaded Fran. "It's still early. The sun is barely up. They won't be open for another half hour."

"We have to do it before anybody sees us. If anyone does, you know what will happen. They'll arrest us and take him away to be euthanized," responded Chris, removing the child carrier from the car.

"Love you, Joshua," sobbed Fran, as her husband took the baby to the entrance of the building.

* * *

The Morgans returned home and the following week executed the second part of their plan, which involved reporting to the authorities that they took the life of their child to prevent the state from doing so.

"You threw your baby into the Chesapeake Bay to keep us from terminating him? How is that more humane than what we do, medicate an infant so he or she simply goes to sleep?" asked an official at the State Adjustment Center (SAC).

"We wanted him to be with us, his parents, when he passed away. Not be disposed of like so much rubbish by unfeeling bureaucrats," explained Fran, caustically.

"Oh, and dumping him from a bridge wasn't treating him like rubbish?" replied the SAC official, snidely.

"No, we loved him and wanted him to leave this earth with us, not strangers who could not care less about his life," countered Fran.

"It's not *his* life that's the main concern. It's the lives of all of those innocent people he would have harmed when he grew up," retorted the state official.

"He was a good baby and would have been a good adult," spit Fran, defiantly.

"Parents are so easily deluded in such matters. They simply can't see the reality of the situation, which as it now exists requires that this be investigated. During this period, you will be asked to remain in your home. If you do not, you shall be incarcerated until the matter is settled."

A month passed before the Morgans were allowed to move about freely.

"We have been unable to find the body of your child, because the currents are simply too strong in the Chesapeake. That is, if the baby was disposed of in the manner you say. To date, we have interviewed your family, friends, and associates, and your story has been corroborated. That said, the investigation will continue until the state is satisfied with your claim," proclaimed the SAC official.

* * *

Many years passed during which the Morgans decided against having another child for fear it, too, would have a grave neurological disorder. As they settled into late middle age, the child they had lost became less prominent in their thoughts. When they did think of him, they wondered if he had become the madman the INI predicted. While the number of serial killings had dropped significantly since infants were tested for genetic flaws, they had not been eradicated. The government attributed this to babies slipping through the system because of uncooperative parents.

"Do you think we did the right thing?" contemplated Fran again, after seeing another news report about the murders of several women.

"Too late to question now what you wanted then," replied Chris.

"You didn't want him euthanized either . . . did you?"

"Of course not. But maybe we put our own interests ahead of others. I mean, what if he turned out the way they said he would. The chances were good he would. That makes us responsible for anything he's done," answered Chris, staring at Joshua's baby picture on the fireplace mantel.

"He'd be thirty-six this week, Chris."

"I know . . . on the 14th. Hard to believe so much time has passed."

"It's also hard to believe he's a psychopath," said Fran, gazing at the floor.

"We can't dwell on this, honey. It will just drive us nuts," replied Chris, looking away from his son's picture.

* * *

The week before their son would turn forty years old, the Morgans received a letter that put them in a tailspin.

Dear Mother and Father,

I know you will be shocked to hear from me, your son, Joshua. It has taken me years to find you. How I learned of your existence and whereabouts is a long and complicated story. The important thing to me is that I have located my birth parents. I have so many questions and hope it will be all right if I visit you next Monday, which happens to be my birthday.

See you then.
Joshua

"Oh, my God! He's coming here. We'll see our son," said Fran, excitedly.

"No return address, but the envelope is postmarked Seattle," observed Chris.

"What's the matter? Aren't you happy?"

"I just can't believe it. After nearly forty years and he found us? He's alive, and we're going to see him."

"What about the authorities?" asked Fran, suddenly looking concerned.

"Hon, you think they're still monitoring us after nearly four decades? Believe me, we're long since in SAC's closed file.

"Oh, thank heavens," sighed Fran.

"Seattle. That's where they've been having all those . . . serial killings. Isn't it?"

"What do you mean?" asked Fran, curiously.

"The postmark. It's Seattle. Look."

As Fran examined the envelope, her expression grew dark.

"You don't think its Joshua? My heavens," responded Fran, alarmed.

"I don't know... I *just* don't know. But it's strange we suddenly get a letter from Joshua and he happens to be living in Seattle."

"Do you think he hates us for giving him up? He doesn't know why... that we were trying to save him," inquired Fran, her apprehension growing.

"Maybe he wants revenge," said Chris after a long pause. "Could be he *is* homicidal, and he's harbored anger for us all these years."

"What should we do?" asked Fran, shivering. "Go to the police?"

"And, what? Tell them our son, the one we supposedly drowned, the one that they wanted to euthanize because of a brain defect, is alive? They'd put us in jail, and shoot him on the spot," answered Chris, pacing the living room.

"We have to think of something before he arrives and harms us—or anyone else," wailed Fran, wringing her hands.

* * *

Convinced their sole offspring was intent on adding them to his list of victims, the Morgans decided on a preemptive strike. They devised a plan wherein they would ambush him when he entered their house—smashing his skull with a blunt instrument. After putting him down, they would call the police claiming a stranger had broken into their home and threatened them with violence.

When their doorbell rang Monday, they were prepared to do what they believed was necessary for their continued existence and that of others. If Joshua was the Seattle serial killer—and they believed he was—they had a responsibility to remove him from society. After all, they had sired him and made it possible for him to grow to adulthood.

The thin figure that stood before them was not what they expected. There was nothing threatening about him. In fact, his warm smile was instantly disarming, and it shook their resolve.

"Hello," said their son, tentatively, and all of the apprehension the Morgans' had felt melted away.

"Joshua?" asked Fran, staring at a person who looked like a younger version of her husband.

"Mom?" answered Joshua, spreading his arms to hug her.

For several moments, the Morgans and the son they had not seen for a lifetime embraced in the foyer of the house.

"Come in, son . . . please," said Chris, wiping tears from his eyes.

"I can't believe it's you. I knew you weren't a serial . . ." sniffled Fran, catching herself before completing the horrible term.

Hours passed as the reunited family sat together on the living room couch and recounted their respective pasts.

Joshua told of his life as a financial analyst, how he had yet to meet a woman he cared to marry, and the energy efficient home he helped build north of Seattle.

"It's nice and private. No neighbors to bug me. I'm not a real people person."

"How long will you be here in D.C.? I hope we can have a nice long visit," gushed Fran, rubbing her son's arm affectionately.

"Not long, I'm afraid. I just came here to see the parents that gave me away when I was a baby."

"What?" asked Fran, suddenly wounded.

"But, we told you why," objected Chris, shaken.

"I have something for you," said Joshua, removing a knife from under his jacket. "I've wanted to give you this forever."

Fast Food

The biggest attraction at Jacob's restaurant

was its flying servers.

While the food at the small bistro was quite good,

the service was outstanding.

Things Are What They Seem

Humankind cannot bear very much reality
—T.S. Eliot

When the leaves turned and started falling in mid-July, Rufus sensed there was trouble brewing. Even in northern Canada, the deciduous trees did not usually change color for another six weeks. *The weather wasn't the cause*, Rufus figured, as it had been a warmer than usual summer. But the land was looking autumnal. The small ground animals were behaving out of season too, scurrying about for food to store away for the not so imminent winter. *Something was out of whack*, Rufus thought, as he stood on the porch of his small log cabin. But the explanation for whatever might be happening eluded him and that made him anxious.

His concern grew when the usually abundant supply of fish in the nearby lake seemed to have suddenly disappeared. For three days he tried to hook a meal but had to settle for trapped rabbit, which did not please his palate nearly as much as rainbow trout. Compounding his dissatisfaction was the recent bitter taste of his quarry. While hare was not his favorite dish, Rufus found that when it was roasted to a crispy finish it had better flavor. He particularly liked the crunch of the skin, which he doused in a generous concoction of seasonings, foremost among them hot sauce and honey. Now, however, nothing overcame the strong acidic taste of the cooked rabbit. He noticed, too, that it was tougher and more chewy than usual. All and all, it was not very rewarding chow, as far as Rufus was concerned.

As if this was not enough, the vegetables from his small garden also tasted peculiar. Not bad or disgusting, just different . . . kind of sugary. He didn't particularly mind that, but it did add to his feeling that nature was out of sorts and not herself. He went to bed worrying about all these inexplicable changes, which combined to keep him awake. When the clock on the fireplace mantel reached midnight, he threw in the towel and got up. To Rufus, it was a waste of time to remain in bed without sleeping, so he decided to have a smoke. He collected his pipe and headed to the porch, but the brilliant sunlight that poured into the cabin when he opened the door stopped him in his tracks.

"What the holy goddamn shit is going on?" he blurted, covering his eyes.

At first Rufus thought he was dreaming and then he realized he was quite conscious. Something else caught his attention that completely jarred him. In the small opening to the woods, across a field from his house, was a group of animals facing in his direction. It was not unusual to see wildlife where he lived, quite the contrary, but this gathering of creatures was bizarre. In the middle of a cluster of raccoons, squirrels, and rabbits sat a large grizzly bear. It made no attempt to attack what was its usual prey. In fact, the small furry creatures scampered and hopped around the bear as if it didn't exist. As Rufus watched in disbelief, two grey foxes joined the group. They approached the bear and touched its nose with theirs in what seemed a greeting. Their comradely act was followed by the grizzly's long tongue licking their tapered snouts.

Rufus rubbed his eyes hoping the absurd scene would dissolve, but it did not. It got even stranger when a huge human figure adorned in a suit of armor—like some kind of knight out of King Arthur's court—emerged from the forest and waved his gauntlet. On impulse, he returned the gesture, and the figure

OF NIGHT AND LIGHT

moved in his direction.

"Oh, jeez," muttered Rufus, quickly retreating behind the cabin door and locking it.

I got to be seeing things. Had too much moonshine last night, mulled Rufus, as he went to the window and parted the canvas that covered it.

"Lord have mercy, he's coming this way!" whimpered Rufus, grabbing for his shotgun, which he always kept loaded.

Rufus then moved to the interior of the one room dwelling prepared to take a stand should the ironclad giant break in. As he stood in the dark, he noticed a flickering light move about the room.

"What the . . .?" he mumbled, reaching for his flashlight.

He moved its beam in pursuit of the flying object and then finally managed to catch up to it. What he saw made the hair on the back of his neck stand on end. Suspended near the topmost rafter of his cabin was a tiny human form with colorful translucent wings.

"A goddamn fairy!" he bellowed, skeptically.

The sight of it caused him to drop his Eveready, leaving only the illumination cast by the airborne object. Rufus felt around in the dark but could not retrieve his flashlight. He then unsuccessfully searched his pants for a match to ignite.

As Rufus struggled in the dark, he heard footsteps mount the stairs to his porch.

"Who's there?" he shouted. "Scat!! You better get out of here right now before I unload this shotgun at you."

"Hold on," returned a voice, which at first did not sound familiar to Rufus. "It's Myles. Come on and open the darn door."

"Okay, okay," replied Rufus, finally realizing it was his brother.

"What's going on here, Rufus? You losing it? Better put that gun down before you shoot someone . . . like me, for instance."

Rufus stared at his sibling but was unable to speak. There was something horribly strange about him, too. And then he realized what it was. His brother's mouth was on his forehead.

"What's the matter, big brother? You look like you're seeing a ghost."

"Your mouth, it's . . ." stammered Rufus.

"It's *what*?" replied Myles, shrugging his shoulders.

"It's not where it should be," answered Rufus, pointing toward the top of his brother's face.

"Whoa! What's going on with you? Let's get some light in here. Maybe your sight is off," remarked Myles, parting the curtains on the cabin's two windows.

Rufus looked outside and saw the grizzly and its small companions still romping around at the woods' edge, but the armored figure was nowhere to be seen.

"They're still out there," reported Rufus, peering outside. Damned if they ain't still there, 'cept the knight."

"Huh? I don't see a darn thing, unless you're talking about the trees and stuff, and that ain't unusual," replied Myles, gaping out of the window.

Rufus lifted the shotgun, aiming in the direction of the phantasm, but his brother took it from him.

"Okay, I think we best get you to see somebody. Maybe go into town. Could be you got something going on with your eyes . . . or *something*," said Myles, leading his compliant brother from the cabin.

Three hours later, as dusk descended, Rufus was being examined at the Moison, Manitoba, medical facility, while his brother awaited word on his condition.

"So you've been seeing strange things, Mr. Randall?" asked the young attending physician, Dr. Cabot.

"I'll say. Seen a grizzly playing with little critters they usually eat and a giant

OF NIGHT AND LIGHT

in full body armor. And my brother's mouth was not where it should be. Actually, yours ain't either."

"I see. Where exactly is my mouth?"

Rufus moved closer to the physician's face.

"You don't have one . . . wait, I think I see it, but it's awful small. Kind of like a peep hole."

"I see. Well, is it where it should be, Mr. Randall?"

"I guess it is," Rufus replied, hesitantly.

"That's progress, I suppose you could say. Why don't you just rest here while I arrange for a couple of tests to make sure you're all right," advised Cabot, placing his stethoscope against Rufus' carotid artery again.

As the doctor checked his vital signs, Rufus glanced out of the window.

"The moon is out," observed Rufus, as the doctor returned his stethoscope to his jacket.

"Moon?"

"Yes, the moon is out," replied Rufus, nodding toward the window.

"Oh, yeah . . . *the* moon. I'll be right back, Mr. Randall. You just relax, okay? We'll get to the bottom of this."

Dr. Cabot found Myles Randall in the waiting room and gave him an update.

"The good news is I don't detect anything physically wrong with your brother, but he's clearly at least somewhat delusional."

"Oh? How so? Did he claim your mouth was in the wrong place?"

"Well, no, but he only sees *one* moon," replied the doctor.

Back in his room, Rufus peered out of the window and wondered if there were always two faces of men in the moon.

Probably never noticed, he mumbled to himself, as his eyes grew heavy. *At least their mouths are in the right place.*

Barely

*We are ashamed of everything that is real about us. . .
just as we are asheamed of our naked skins.*
—George Bernard Shaw

Jason Conway climbed from the shower at 6:28 A.M., quickly dried himself, and slipped on his boxers. At 6:30 the t-shirt he attempted to pull over his head flew from his hands and landed on the head of his wife, who was sitting naked on the commode.

"Very funny, Jason," mumbled Lacy Conway, from beneath the cotton garment.

"I didn't do that," protested Jason.

"Oh, sure. It just landed here on its own," replied Lacy, throwing the t-shirt to her husband.

Again, Jason attempted to pull the undershirt over his head, and again it sprung from his hands, this time landing atop the hamper.

"I saw that!" exclaimed Lacy. "What the hell are you doing?"

"Nothing! I didn't throw it. It jumps away every time I try to put it on."

"Stop goofing around and get out of the bathroom. I have to take my shower."

"I'm not goofing around," grumbled Jason, grabbing his t-shirt from the top of the hamper and leaving the bathroom.

He tried to pull the undergarment over his head three more times, but each time it sprung away as if invisible hands were yanking it from him.

"*What the hell . . .,*" Jason growled, kicking it across the bedroom and fishing another undershirt from his dresser.

Before he attempted to put on the new t-shirt, he decided to slip into his trousers, but the unseen power that had denied him use of his t-shirt yanked them from his legs as soon as he started to raise them to his waist.

"Damn!! This isn't funny!" he bellowed in frustration.

Again, he tried to put on his pants, but it wasn't happening. Before they reached his knees, they were airborne, flying to the other side of the room. As Jason sat on the bed dazed by the bizarre event, he heard his wife cursing loudly in the bathroom.

"What's the matter, honey?" he called, moving swiftly to the bathroom door and opening it.

Inside he found his wife standing on top of the toilet bowl grabbing for her bra, which hung from the ceiling. Her panties dangled near the light fixture a few feet away.

"They won't go on!" she repeated, frantically. "They fly off just like your undershirt did."

"Come on down, Lacy. You'll fall. Something's going on. Maybe we got a . . .,"

"A *what*?" snapped Lacy, dismounting the commode.

Jason led her from the bathroom by the hand, and they both plopped down on the edge of their bed.

"I can't put on my pants either. They just keep coming off," said Jason, reaching for his socks and sliding one onto his foot.

It moved around like a hand puppet and then shot across the floor landing against the closet door.

"Oh my God," said Lacy, whimpering.

"Put on your robe, honey. You look like you're freezing."

Lacy sat staring at the sock with her mouth agape. Jason fetched her bathrobe from the back of the wingback chair next to his wife's bureau and swung it over her shoulders. It immediately sprung from his hands and flew upward into the ceiling fan where it became entangled in its rotating blades.

"Shit! This goddamn house is haunted," shouted Jason, reaching for the switch to stop the fan.

Lucy jumped from the bed and ran to her closet.

"This is freakin' crazy!" she screamed, pulling dresses from their hangers and desperately attempting to put them on without success.

While she struggled to cover her body, Jason did the same in his adjacent closet. In a matter of minutes, heaps of clothes covered their bedroom floor.

"Nothing . . . nothing stays on," pouted Lacy.

"Pick something," ordered Jason, pointing at the mounds. Maybe we can dress in another part of the house . . . or the garage. There's got to be a magnetic field or something messing with the air molecules in here."

The Conways grabbed items from the piles of clothes and scampered from the room. In the hall they attempted to attire themselves, but the garments continued to resist their efforts.

"Try the living room," shouted Jason, but the results were the same there. "The garage. Let's go to the garage."

"It's freezing in here," complained Lacy, bumping against their Toyota Highlander.

"Never mind that. See if you can put your dress on," snapped Jason.

Despite all of their attempts, their clothes would not stay on their chilled bodies.

"Oh, Jason, what are we going to do? We can't leave the house naked. Nobody can see us this way," sobbed Lacy.

"I know," said Jason, sympathetically.

"And my hair. I brush it but it just goes back to this," she said, pointing to the disheveled mop on her head.

"I have to call work and let them know I won't be in," said Jason, following his wife back into the house.

"What are you going to tell them?"

"That we need an exorcism," replied Jason, pressing a button on his cellphone.

After five rings, he reached his company's answering machine. *Where was the receptionist?* Jason wondered. She was always there by 8:30, and it was almost 9:00. *By now he would be arriving at work, too. If things were normal, but they were far from normal,* he thought, with rapidly mounting trepidation.

It was after 10 A.M. when someone besides the recorded voice responded to Jason's phone call.

"Alice isn't here, so I'm fielding calls. Only two other people came in. Seems we're the only ones that were fully clothed when it happened," declared Mark Howard from marketing.

"When *what* happened?" inquired Jason.

"They're not sure, but it seems around 6:30 this morning, if people weren't already dressed, they stayed that way. If you had some of your clothes on, you kept them, but you couldn't put on anything else after that. You were stuck the way you were. So a lot of people are either half naked or totally naked. They think it might be an anti-matter thing, whatever that means. It's all over the news."

Jason hung up and hit the TV remote. The headline across the bottom of the screen read:

COUNTRY IN STATE OF UNDRESS AS CLOTHES DEFY USE.

A reporter gave the details:
So far it appears that the vast majority of the population has remained inside their homes, having lost the ability to dress. Scientists are at a loss to explain why people are not able to put on their clothes. The White House indicates that the Vice President will soon address the country on the matter. This raises the question about the President's own state of dress. The Commander-in-Chief has yet to be seen.

Lacy let out a scream. "What am I going to do? I'm totally naked. At least you have shorts on."

"Oh, and like I want to be seen in these," said Jason, snapping the waistband of his boxers emblazoned with rubber duckies.

"Better than nothing. I'm so cold. Put up the heat," ordered Lacy, collapsing onto the couch and attempting to cover herself with a pillow that flapped away from her.

For the balance of the day, the news was filled with accounts of partially or totally naked celebrities, among them government officials, professional athletes, and film stars. All occupations suffered from shortages of personnel. Services were cut back as businesses lacked the employees to continue normal operation. Life was grinding to a halt as unclothed humans chose to remain out of sight. The world faced a growing quandary.

* * *

A week into the dilemma, the Conways were nearly out of food, and they were not alone in that situation. Delivery services were overwhelmed, since their ranks, too, had been drastically reduced by what was now being called "The Undress" by the media. Speculation about the cause was rampant. The most popular theory was posited by the Center for Extraterrestrial Studies, which held that aliens were likely conducting an experiment or enjoying a joke at the expense of Earthlings. In the end, most people felt there was no plausible explanation for what had happened at 6:30 in the morning on the 25th of October.

Among the Conways' relatives and friends, only two had been fully attired when The Undress occurred. Lacy's brother, always an early riser, was already at work when most of the country's population was preparing to greet the day. She had spoken to him on the phone, and he had agreed to grocery shop for them. Meanwhile, Jason's best friend and avid jogger, Perry Myles, had visited and, likewise, agreed to assist the Conways in any way he could. Despite the bizarre nature of the situation, Perry could not conceal his amusement over the predicament confronting half the world.

"My boss can't leave the house either. Naked as a jaybird, and that's not a pretty sight considering how fat he is. Hey, like the rubber duckies, buddy."

"Better than nothing," snapped Jason.

"No offense, but this whole thing is pretty hysterical when you think about it."

"Yeah, it's real funny not being able to leave the house or have a normal life. You have any idea how this is going to change everything?"

"It already is changing everything. I'm in charge of the dealership now. Of course, car sales are off big time, because so many people can't go any place. You should see the highways. Traffic is way down. Like a holiday out there. Things have pretty much come to a halt. You been watching the news?"

"That's all I've been doing," responded Jason, nodding toward the television.

"Well, it's a hell of a lot more peaceful in the world. All quiet on the war fronts, they say. Guess naked soldiers don't like it when their guns are exposed," chuckled Perry.

"I can't see the humor in any of it. Things are crumbling, man. Wall Street is in the dumpster and they say there's going to be massive shortages in everything from medicine to milk. Not so funny, pal," replied Jason, glumly.

"Sorry, I'm just trying to make light of a bad situation. I guess it's easier for me to do that when I'm not bare ass. I try not to dwell on what's happening, because it's scary as shit. I mean, why would aliens do something like this, and who knows what they'll do next?"

"Not sure I buy the ET theory. Why the hell would they do something like this?"

"Maybe they're laughing their asses off up there on Mars."

"No one knows what's going on. Not even the so-called experts. All anyone knows is things are really screwed up."

"Well, I, for one, think the VP looked pretty damn cute in his PJs. You see him? I almost crapped myself. No sign of the First Lady either. Maybe she's like Lacy. *Hey Lacy, come on out. Not good form hiding from your company*," yelled Perry, winking at Jason.

"Drop dead!" replied Lacy, hiding in the kitchen.

"People are just going to have to get over their inhibitions if things are going to get back on track," observed Perry, turning serious for a moment.

"Don't see that happening any time soon," replied Jason, escorting his friend to the door.

"I'll get the stuff you want in case the power goes out, but the utility companies say they have enough personnel to keep things fired up."

"I'm not that confident. The lights have already been flickering. Don't want to be left in the dark. Appreciate it, Perry."

"No problem, bro. You better get back inside before the neighborhood sees your duckies," said Perry, pointing to Jason's shorts.

"Shit," replied Jason, suddenly aware he was standing on his front steps in full view of a passing school bus that appeared half-empty.

* * *

It took the Conways two nights to figure out how to cover themselves in bed. After non-stop battles with flying blankets, Jason inserted a piece of two-by-four between the mattress and box spring so they could burrow between them to keep warm. Even with the thermostat cranked up to almost 80 degrees, Lacy still complained of being cold.

"So this is how we're going to live our lives?" she lamented over the phone to her mother, who also had emerged from the shower at the fateful moment when humans were no longer able to clothe themselves.

"Your father had his robe on, but nothing under it and no socks or slippers. He's had to fetch wood for the fireplace barefoot. Stepped on something and cut his foot. We called Dr. Peters' office, but there was no answer. He's probably naked like the rest of us. The cut looks better though, so I don't think it's a big deal."

"Can you and daddy come over after it gets dark? I'm bored and lonely," Lacy pleaded.

"Oh, I don't think I'd dare leave the house without clothes on, honey. Maybe daddy can come by. I'll check with him when he wakes up from his nap, okay?"

Later in the day, Lacy's mother called back and reported that her father had no intention of venturing out in public in his old robe, adding that his foot was too sore to walk on anyway. This news deepened Lacy's gloom, and she climbed between the mattress and box spring and sobbed.

As he had for days, Jason sat in the living room glued to CNN. Nudists around the country had seized The Undress to expound on the virtues of their lifestyle, suggesting that it was the answer to the dilemma confronting the world. A female reporter clad only in a bra and slip asked the director of the American Naturism Society to explain:

> There's nothing more natural in the world than the human body. Covering it is a perversion of what nature intended. We praise the beauty of the stallion and lion, but are their forms concealed by fabrics? Of course they're not. Discarding clothes liberates us and returns us to our purest state. Besides, it's healthy, comfortable, and relaxing. Nothing worse than getting all sticky and knotted up in underpants on a steamy, summer day.

The concept made sense to Jason, but he had to admit that the idea of living in a world where everyone was naked would take some getting used to. It surprised him when a growing number of government officials and prominent figures suggested that nudism might be the solution to The Undress. Religious leaders, except for those in the Catholic Church, were adamantly opposed to the revolutionary proposal. Rumors circulated that the Pope was caught naked at the hour of The Undress, explaining why the world's largest Christian sect was not averse to the notion.

* * *

As the debate continued, a small percentage of the population embraced nudism as the answer to the problem. It gradually became common to encounter a naked person striding down a street or shopping for groceries. At first some early converts to nudism were met with hostility, but as it became more and more apparent that no other solution to the crisis existed, resistance faded. Still, the majority of those caught short at the moment of The Undress remained secreted from public view.

A sudden, unexpected event substantially changed that. As the Conways snuggled before the television, Wolf Blitzer announced an important news update from Washington. The screen switched to the large double-doors that concealed the long red-carpeted corridor in the White House. When the entrance opened millions of viewers beheld the stark-naked figure of the President of the United States as he strode to a waiting podium.

Light and Matter

Image, that flying still before me, gleamed
Upon the glassy plain.
—William Wordsworth

"It could be related to the Large Wendover Collider out on the Flats," offered Dr. Joe Venning of the Sabra Medical Institute. "Mr. Drake was out there doing field strength readings for the Holbrook antenna on the 21st when they reported a fault."

"What are you suggesting?" asked Dr. Sam Dorman, Director of Nuclear Medicine at the South Ogden facility. "We have no research that indicates collider particle escape does anything to those in its path."

"Well, that's because there's no empirical data on the subject, and you know there's been some concern. Parameters are being established to study it."

As Venning and Dorman considered the situation regarding Liam Drake, he lay with a blindfold over his eyes on the couch in the living room of his modest split level ten miles away. Four days earlier, Drake's vision had suddenly become impaired and since then his world alternated between darkness and an infinite array of pulsing and throbbing geometric forms that reminded him of a poster he once owned in his college days.

Life on an acid trip, mused Liam, peeking out from under his blindfold to see if anything had changed. It had not. The first evidence of his ocular odyssey came in the form of thick ascending horizontal lines that appeared as he returned to his vehicle on the northeast edge of the Great Salt Flats after logging the signal readings he needed. It seemed as if he'd entered an M.C. Escher painting, one of those titled stairwells, and he quickly became both disoriented and light-headed.

He managed to reach the highway, at which point he could no longer see past the barrage of iridescent planes that totally obscured his sight. He felt around and located his cellphone and called his office.

"Bill? Hey, man, I got a problem out here. I'm at the entrance to Service Road 18 and can't see a thing. I mean besides a crazy light show. Bright colors flashing every which way. If I shut my eyes, they go away, but when I open them it's like I'm in some kind of freaky kaleidoscope. I don't know what's happening. Maybe I'm having a stroke or something."

"Okay, Liam, just relax. I'll be out there within an hour. Can you wait? Maybe you should call 911," suggested Bill Wyman, Holbrook Communications chief engineer.

"No... no. I don't want that whole drama. Besides, it's only my eyes. I don't have any other symptoms. No pain or numbness," Liam responded.

"Good, but if you do get any other symptoms, call 911."

"It would take them as long to get here as you, so please do come get me. Probably be fine by then anyway."

When Wyman arrived at the scene, Liam's condition had not worsened, but it had not improved either.

"Let's get you to the ER, buddy. This is pretty weird," observed Wyman, helping Liam from his truck.

"Came on me out there," reported Liam, pointing his finger behind him. "Writing down field strengths and then 'Bam!' and I'm inside a lava lamp.

Could just see enough to drive this far before I lost all of my vision. Could see only these lights and lines . . . hundreds of them zigzagging every which way. Like nothing I've ever experienced."

* * *

By the time they reached the Sabre Medical Institute emergency room, Liam was more concerned that he was in deep trouble. Nothing had improved during the hour ride. In fact, if anything the optical illusion had become more overwhelming and at times it felt as if it would suffocate him. The only way he could relieve his mounting anxiety was to keep his eyes tightly shut.

"Everything appears okay. Pupils a bit dilated," reported the ER physician, shining a light into Liam's eyes. "Otherwise things look pretty normal . . . slight ocular hypertension. We'll do a CAT scan."

In minutes, Liam was wheeled into the imaging room. An hour later, he met with a neurologist.

"Your scan shows a little pressure on the cranial nerve but nothing exceptional. Did you look at the sun for an extended period? Did you encounter any kind of bright flash out on the desert?" inquired Dr. Casey. "These can cause a spasm in the peripheral nervous system which can manifest in visual distortion. They're generally short lived . . . maybe lasting a few minutes, not hours like yours."

"I wear sunglasses whenever I'm outside, especially out on the flats," answered Liam, now wearing a blindfold provided by the hospital.

"Well, we'll do a few more tests and go from there. You say you're feeling no physical discomfort other than the queasiness that the hallucinations cause you? Anxiety, right?"

"Yeah, it's freaking me out, but no pain."

"We'll keep you overnight until we get the results of the tests. Things should calm down by then. Hang in there. We'll give you something to help you relax."

* * *

The next morning while Liam lay in darkness in his hospital room, Dr. Casey greeted him with the results of his additional scans.

"I've got good news, and I have less good news. The good news is that there is nothing exceptional about your tests. Everything is quite normal. And thus the less good news is that we simply don't know what is causing your problem."

"So what's next?" asked Liam, lifting the blindfold. "Shit!" he blurted, replacing it. "Same fireworks show. A psychedelic tsunami, Doc. What can be done? It's over for me if this doesn't go away."

"I think you should go to the Mayo Clinic for further tests. They have top eye and brain people there. Maybe they can make sense of this."

As he spoke, Dr. Venning entered the room.

"Hi Joe. This is our mystery patient," said Dr. Casey. "Mr. Drake, meet Dr. Venning. He has a few questions he'd like to ask you. While he's doing that I'll see if I can arrange a visit to the Mayo, okay?"

"I guess," replied Liam, feeling his life drift further out of his control.

"Hello, Mr. Drake. I hope you don't mind, but I'd like to ask you a few things."

"Sure, go ahead. I'm not going anywhere. What do you want to ask? Do I take drugs? No. Do I often see things that aren't there? No. Do I . . .."

"When you were out working on the flats yesterday, did you notice anything peculiar . . . like unusual sounds? Feel any vibrations or tremors?"

"No . . . no noises or shaking, but come to think of it I saw this . . . this wave."

"Wave?" asked Venning.

"Kind of like a mirage. You know, when you look out on the desert and you see everything gyrating or wiggling. This was different though. It was right in front of me. Like this far, maybe," said Liam, holding his hand a foot from his face.

"Then what?" Venning asked, captivated by Liam's account.

"Went by in a second. Swoosh. Just like that," answered Liam, again demonstrating with his hand. "I thought I might be tearing up. Sometimes sand gets in my eyes, and it causes them to get all watery. Then the world looks like it's in a fish bowl."

"So everything appeared warped or deformed?" inquired Venning, taking notes.

"Yeah, but I knew it wasn't sand in my eyes. No wind blowing at all."

"And that's when you started seeing the bright objects?"

"Pretty much . . . within a couple of minutes. I was heading to my pickup when I saw this green line floating in front of me. At first I thought it was something real and I reached out for it, but I couldn't feel anything. Then another one appeared above it and another above that, and they were all different colors, orange and purple. Pretty soon there were dozens of them spiraling around. Looked like a staircase. Before long there were other things floating in all directions, and they were moving vertically and horizontally. Just managed to reach route 196. It wasn't long before I couldn't see anything but those shapes, and they were in all sizes and really bright. When I looked harder, I could tell they were moving . . . not stationary. But traveling at warp speed. Maybe at the speed of light, if you can detect that kind of movement. Fast, that's all I know. Not only did they move around and by me, but they moved through me."

"Really? Could you feel them?" asked Venning.

"Not at all. But it was creepy, I can tell you that."

"I can imagine."

Liam heard someone enter the room.

"They'll release you in about an hour. Who'll be picking you up?" inquired Dr. Casey.

"My brother. He lives next door to me."

"Good. We're in touch with Mayo to get you an appointment. We'll call you when things are firmed up. In the meantime, here's a prescription for eye drops I want you to use twice a day. It will relieve your optical hypertension, which we noted in the last test. If anything changes, get in touch with us immediately."

* * *

Brian Drake drove his brother home and helped him settle in.

"Just stay on the couch, and I'll bring your food. It's a straight line to the john. I'm moving this chair out of your path, so just take twenty steps to your right, and there you are."

"Thanks, Brian. I know the layout, so I'm good. Cellphone's right here, and the TV remote, too. Not that I could watch it, but I got my iPod to keep me company. Don't worry. I'll be all right, unless this thing takes a turn for the worse and these objects take tangible form. Then I'm screwed."

"Not likely, man. Eyes play tricks on all of us for one reason or another. You'll be fine," assured his younger sibling.

For the next two days, Liam remained couch bound and had frequent visits from his doting brother who delivered enough food to sate the appetites of contestants on *The Biggest Loser*.

"You got to keep your strength up," said Brian when Liam balked at the enormity of the meals he brought.

"At this rate I'll need a triple bypass before I even get to the Mayo Clinic."

It was late on day two that Liam realized he was beginning to enjoy the light show in his head. There was something soothing, if not mesmerizing, about it. The colors appeared more vibrant than ever and the objects more numerous. To amuse himself, Liam attempted to name the geometric forms as they appeared. As it happened, math was his second major in college and for a time he had considered pursuing a graduate degree in the discipline rather than take the engineering job at Holbrook.

Okay, thought Liam with his blindfold off, *that's a rectangle, decagon, triangle, heptagon . . . no, it's a hexagon. There's a trapezoid, pentagon, square, bunch of circles, more triangles, parallelogram, cross . . .*

When Liam's brother showed up with his evening banquet, he found his brother lost in his interior pyrotechnics. It took several minutes for Liam to respond to Brian's queries.

"It's amazing . . . really amazing," he responded.

"You had me scared, Liam. Why's the blindfold off?"

"This is exceptional. It's like seeing the world reduced to its elemental forms. There's something special about this, Brian."

"What do you mean? I thought it was freaking you out. Now you sound like you're into it. Maybe we should call Dr. Casey. He said to let him know if anything changed. I think this qualifies as a change, bro."

"No, it's good. Don't worry. I'm fine," replied Liam, drifting in his reverie. "There's another trapezoid . . . and a quadrilateral. Whoa, just flew over my head. Can't even describe the color."

"You haven't eaten lunch, man," remarked Brian, with deepening concern. "You always dig Carrie's chicken salad."

Liam said nothing.

"Hey, you hearing me in there? Liam . . . Liam?"

"Sublime . . . totally sublime," responded Liam.

"Your eyes look weird. The pupils are tiny, and they're red . . . no blue. Shit, they're changing color," noted Brian, his face inches from his brother's.

Liam began to giggle like a delighted child. After further attempts to gain the attention of his sibling, Brian called 911, and within a half hour they were back at the hospital. Shortly after their arrival, Dr. Casey was on the scene accompanied by Dr. Venning.

"Mr. Drake? Can you hear me?" asked Casey, inspecting Liam's eyes. "Jeez, never seen this. Take a look, Joe."

"His pupils are nearly gone," responded Venning. "Let's get him to imaging now."

* * *

Both doctors and Brian stood behind the technician in the imagining room while he took shots of Liam's brain.

"What the hell is that behind his visual cortex?" blurted Venning.

"Looks like a . . . a peace symbol. Damn thing's changing colors. This is bizarre!"

"Has to be related to the Wendover Collider exudation," observed Venning. "Can you get Dr. Dorman up here?"

When Dorman arrived, Venning ordered Liam's images transferred to the room's widescreen monitor.

"What the . . .? You photo shop these?" asked Dorman in disbelief.

"It's real and growing. When we first noticed it, it was quite small. It's tripled in size since."

"It looks like a . . . ."

"Peace sign?" interrupted Venning.

"Come on guys. Good joke. Let me see a live image," requested Dorman.

The screen displayed Liam's brain as he lay in the scanner.

"Jesus," muttered Dorman. "Okay, let's get him to isolation. Could be contagious."

"We need to airlift him to Mayo right away," said Casey, grabbing the imaging room phone.

"I want to go with him," interjected Brian, fear pinching his expression.

"Fine. I'll come along, too," responded Venning.

* * *

In less than an hour, Liam, his brother, and Venning were airborne and dressed in hazardous material suits, as was the plane's crew.

"Liam . . . Liam, can you hear me?" asked Brian, sounding as if his hands were cupped over his mouth.

He got no response.

"His vitals are pretty stable. Every so often there's a spike in his EKG," observed Venning.

"Why is that?" inquired Brian.

"It's like he's reacting to some kind of stimuli," answered Venning.

"His pupils are completely gone," observed Brian, with heightened urgency.

"I've never seen only irises," added Venning, slipping the blindfold back over Liam's eyes.

The eye covering that had provided Liam relief from his phantasms no longer worked, and that pleased him. He wanted nothing more than to remain in his strange new world.

* * *

By late afternoon, Liam was installed in a special wing in the Mayo Clinic and scheduled for a battery of tests. Both Dr. Venning and Brian were advised to take a break while they awaited the results. Before leaving Liam's side, Brian assured his brother that he would be nearby and that everything would be all right.

Liam heard what sounded like a voice in the far distance but he was focused on the most extraordinary shape he had ever encountered. As it drew near, his pleasure grew, and by the time it reached him he was ecstatic. He had never encountered anything so spectacular . . . so divine. When he reached for it, he found that it was palpable. His entire body tingled with indescribable joy when he made contact with it. He knew then he was where he wanted to spend eternity, and he climbed aboard its magenta surface. "*Oh*," sighed Liam, rapturously. "*Ohh . . . .*"

* * *

Dr. Venning and Brian found a small grassy courtyard just outside Liam's unit. The fresh twilight air felt rejuvenating to them. For several minutes they stood gazing at the darkening horizon.

"Do you see that?" asked Venning, breaking the silence.

"What?" responded Brian, concentrating on the space before him.

"There's this . . . *this* convex object floating just over there. It's changing colors."

"What about that triangle that's . . ." replied Brian, halting midsentence.

"Oh, wow!" said Venning, his arms sweeping the air around him.

"It's so . . . I think they . . ." mumbled Brian.

"Close your eyes. You can block it," suggested Venning.

"No, I can't. I tried that," replied Brian.

"I can't either," said Venning, finding that the throbbing shapes dominated his mind's eye as well.

"That's okay," answered Brian, absorbed. "I like it . . . *so* much."

A prolonged silence ensued before Venning responded. "Me, too. It's wonderful . . . where I always wanted to be."

* * *

From the manned Mars probe fifty million miles away, the ship's crew watched transfixed as Earth flashed brilliantly and then disappeared. As they stared at the point in the sky where their home had once been, a vast array of colored shapes forming a Sangraal emerged from the void and moved toward them. They could not avert their gaze, and they did not wish to try.

Moments passed and then the probe's captain spoke, "It's amazing . . . just *so* incredibly magnificent."

Her crew agreed.

Gloomy Girl

To these my thoughts

return instead

in contemplation

of which I dread

the thought of slumber

deep and dead.

The Lonely Strand

The wilderness and the solitary place shall be glad for them.
—Isaiah

    Only a handful of businesses, among them a barber shop, convenience store, farm supply depot, and pharmacy remained open along the dusty main street of Seymore, Kansas. Every one of them was teetering on the edge of extinction. Just eighteen miles from the Colorado border, the tiny hamlet had seen most of its population move elsewhere or die off. The Miller Grain Cooperative had kept the town afloat for nearly a century, but with its demise a decade earlier, Seymore fell on hard times. Young people fled for opportunities elsewhere, leaving in their wake an aging population to keep the windswept, high plains town on the map. By 1997, the number of residents had slipped to 372 from nearly a thousand two decades earlier.

    As a lifelong resident of Seymore, Josh Emmett had worked in the Miller granary his entire adult life. Though he might otherwise have gone elsewhere when it closed, his disfigurement kept him from setting out to more promising places. His settlement with the company after his accident allowed him to pay off his modest house on the town's edge and meet his daily needs, which were minimal. Josh's only extravagance was an occasional tin of Skoal and a trip over to Goodland for some extra crispy KFC. His was a simple, if not solitary existence. Both parents were gone and his few remaining relatives lived in other parts of the state and places more distant. His childhood friend, Henry Capon, also a former Miller Grain employee, had died of a lung disease he had attributed to his job, although he had been a chain smoker since his teens.

Josh's hopes of living a normal family life ended when his arm and leg were caught in a sweep auger while he was attempting to repair it. While part of his arm remained attached to his body, it hung from his shoulder like a dead tree limb. His right leg had been severed from the knee, and although he was given a prosthetic device, he never used it—preferring to walk with the aid of a crutch. Josh knew whatever appeal he possessed for the ladies was lost that fateful day.

"Not a big market for someone with a three figure bank account that looks like me," he had commented to his cousin in Wichita, and it pretty much summarized his situation.

This was not the future he had envisioned when he was young—these bleak and endless days at age fifty-eight. Alone in his windblown one-bedroom bungalow that stood in the shadow of the abandoned grain silo where he'd earned his living, Josh would reminisce about better times—such as they were. Invariably, his recollections would center on the times he spent in the old Strand Theater viewing movies that nourished his imagination while contributing to a long-standing mystery that came to intrigue and haunt him.

* * *

On different occasions he had witnessed something quite extraordinary and disconcerting. While watching a vampire movie called *Horror of Dracula*, he had seen the actual star, Christopher Lee, standing in a corner next to the stage while his image filled the backdrop. He could not believe what he was seeing and looked harder, shading his eyes from the glare of the screen. What he observed was the actor turning away after a moment and vanishing into the darkness behind him. When he reported this to Henry, he was told he had *bats in his belfry*—a favorite insult of his friend's. His parents said pretty much the same but in kinder words, and, after a while, Josh became convinced that he had, indeed, been seeing things.

He held that belief until he was fourteen when he had another vision in the Strand, but this one was very different from the first. He was not watching a horror movie but rather a romantic comedy, called *Rally 'Round the Flag, Boys,* starring one of his favorite actors, Paul Newman. Midway through the lighthearted flick, one of its young starlets, Tuesday Weld—who instantly captivated Josh with her stunning looks—appeared on the left side of the stage exactly where he had seen Lee years earlier.

Josh jabbed Henry in the shoulder to get his attention, determined this time to verify the bizarre sighting, but his friend was not to be distracted from the celluloid action before him.

"*Shh!*" he snapped, elbowing Josh.

To his surprise, the young Hollywood beauty remained motionless as Josh starred at her. Then his heart jumped in delight as she returned his intense gaze with a seductive smile. Again, he tried to get his friend's attention and again was poked. From his seat in the balcony's front row, Josh followed the beams of smoky light from the projection room down to the screen and understood why Henry was so engrossed. The beguiling ingénue filled the cynosure within the Proscenium Arch. He then moved his eyes back to the incarnate Weld and mouthed the words, "I love you," not expecting a response—but he received one. She returned his amorous declaration, turned, and vanished. He was stunned.

During those fleeting moments, Josh had fallen in love with the film goddess, who he knew was totally unobtainable. Yet he hoped he might meet someone who possessed Weld's qualities, if only minutely. She was his dream girl and rarely left his thoughts, although no one like her ever entered the narrow landscape of his life. Any chance of finding someone even remotely resembling her was lost when he was maimed. After the life-altering incident, he viewed himself as something akin to the monsters in one of the horror movies he'd seen, so he gradually and reluctantly abandoned all hope.

When the Strand finally closed its doors because of declining ticket sales, Josh took it hard. It was as if a vital aspect of his meager existence was taken from him. He had seen all the Tuesday Weld movies at the Strand, and she had appeared in the flesh two more times exactly as she had in the first. Josh loved each of her films, except for one in which the actress was sexually assaulted from the rear by Robert DeNiro in *Once Upon a Time in America*. It made him jealous, but her naked backside aroused him and dominated his thoughts endlessly.

* * *

Memories of the strange events in the town's moving picture hall were never far from his mind, and over the years Josh had examined the outside of the movie house where he calculated Lee and Weld must have exited. In addition to the main entrance, the only door to the building was on the side leading to the parking lot. He recalled its illuminated exit sign above the door inside. He had considered breaking into the Strand but always felt apprehension at the idea. There was something foreboding about the out-of-screen appearances of the actors. *Why had they only appeared to him? What did they want?* he wondered, but then his thoughts reverted to Tuesday Weld and his anxiety would be mitigated by desire.

It was that cherished memory that gave Josh the courage to enter the vacant auditorium. He had to find out what was in the mysterious depths of the corner that provided his visions egress. He waited until after midnight to enter the abandoned cinema and did so by prying the side door with a crowbar. It popped open easily, and a blast of dank air greeted him as he stepped inside. It gave him goose bumps and he stood motionless for a moment. Regaining his courage, he shot the beam of his flashlight across the first floor row of seats and up to the balcony where he had spent so many happy afternoons and evenings in his younger days.

A gust of wind slammed the door behind him and he jumped.

"Shit!" blurted Josh, and then advanced toward his target. To his disappointment, but also a degree of relief, no actors awaited him at the stage's edge. He aimed the shaft of light to the side and noticed a hallway that led to a door.

How was that possible? Josh wondered, moving cautiously toward it. The handle of the door felt warm and moist as if another hand had just been on it. He turned it slowly and then gave the door a slight push. Daylight poured from the small opening.

"What the . . .?" Josh mumbled, stopping to catch his breath.

Bracing himself he pushed the door further and the glare caused him to squint. When he was able to open his eyes fully, he beheld the empty field behind the Strand, but instead of moonlight it was awash in summer sun.

I'm dreaming this. I have to be, he told himself, as the phantom door closed behind him. A figure dressed in black from head to toe stood across the arid clearing. Josh took a few steps forward and then gasped.

"It's her!" Josh uttered in total disbelief. He then shouted her name at the top of his lungs.

From his position, he could just make out a smile on her face, exactly like the one he'd seen before. He began moving toward the object of his desires as quickly as his disabled body would allow. As he neared, she placed the hood of her garment over her head. Tears of joy were running down his cheeks when he arrived at her side.

"Is it you . . . *really* you?" Josh sputtered, breathlessly.

A mocking laugh came from the hooded figure before him.

"Tuesday?" asked Josh, apprehensively.

"You mistake me, sir. My name is Christopher . . . Christopher Lee. You surely remember," said the thespian smiling sardonically as he revealed himself, the red pupils of his eyes aglow.

Josh stepped back. "You're not . . . .."

"Tuesday Weld? Of course I'm not. What did you expect? That was *only* a movie . . . an illusion just like this."

* * *

John Cargill arose from the cot in back of his farm supply store and went outside to relieve himself, since the building's only bathroom was broken. As he stood there emptying his bladder, he noticed the silhouette of a lone figure on the moonlit horizon with his arms outstretched to the heavens. He momentarily wondered who it was, shrugged, and went back inside to bed.

The Chorophobe's Contrition

And he waltzed with a cadaver throught the infinite night
—Curtis Michael Blais

Charley Morse was haunted by the guilt he felt for never having danced with his beloved wife, who now lay dead in the Parkway Funeral Home. During their entire marriage, including their wedding day, he had steadfastly refused to take the floor with her, although she was the love of his life. This always left her disappointed and him feeling like a cad and coward. He simply could not bring himself to shake his booty, as the young people called it, and besides he was certain he had absolutely no sense of rhythm and thus would humiliate himself and his beautiful wife. He believed he had married far above his station and was not about to lower himself further by revealing the oaf he perceived himself to be. Charley never wavered in his conviction even though he sensed it diminished him in his spouse's eyes. This weighed on his conscience and upset him but try as he may he could not change how he felt.

"Come on, let your hair down, you old fart. Let's trip the light fantastic," she would jest attempting to humor him out of his singular inhibition, but as always he proved an immoveable object.

"Oh, you're no fun," she would reply in familiar frustration, a frown replacing her smile, and again he would feel like he had failed her. Even when her cancer had whittled away her once robust frame leaving her with only traces of the vitality and joie de vivre that had so characterized her personality, he refused to waltz to a tune on the radio in their living room where she spent most of her time reclining on a couch.

"How about fulfilling a dying woman's final request?" she asked in little more than a whisper.

"Oh, honey, you can barely stand, and you don't want to make yourself worse, do you?" responded Charley, hoping she would not continue to press him, which he long suspected was her way of avenging his intransigence on the subject.

"You silly man. Who's going to see you?" she had said on that last occasion and those words still rang in his head as he stared through the windshield of his car.

"You will, sweetheart . . . you will," Charley had replied, indeed, feeling every bit the silly man.

"That's okay, dear," she wheezed placing her wilted hand on his, "I still love you anyway."

Two weeks later she was dead and Charley was left with not only a gaping hole in the center of his small universe but an even greater sense that he had been an unforgivably callous and ungenerous man for never giving his wife the one thing she had most wanted from him. Indeed, she had never asked him for anything more. Perhaps because he had provided her with everything a good husband should . . . everything, that is, but the one thing she had desired above all else.

Now he was determined to expunge this blemish from their otherwise perfect union the only way he felt he could. As he watched the funeral home go dark and its staff exit for the night, he gathered up a delicate red rose in his thick hand and climbed from his car. During his wife's wake earlier he had unlocked the window in the men's room with the intention of re-entering the building through it, and that is exactly what he did, boosting his broad haunches over the sill. Once inside, he sat on the commode to catch his breath and regain his focus. He was only a few feet away from where his cherished mate lay in her mahogany coffin and this thought restored his clarity and sense of purpose.

"I'm coming, darling," he whispered as he exited the bathroom and moved in the direction of his awaiting wife.

As he approached the casket, her voice broke the stillness.

"Will you dance with me, Charley?" she asked, and he gently lifted her body off the catafalque to the floor and presented her with the red rose, bowing gallantly.

"Of course, my dearest, I would be delighted to trip the light fantastic with you," he replied, wrapping his arms around her rigid body as tears ran down his cheeks. "There's nothing more I'd rather do."

And in the dim moonlight that spilled into the funeral home's main viewing room, they danced and danced.

The Book Whisperer

Books will speak plain . . .
—Francis Bacon

I can hear the books talking, thought Robin Christopher as he walked by the countless shelves in his personal library. Passing a volume by Robert Frost, for example, he heard, "In three words I can sum up everything I've learned about life: it goes on." *Indeed,* muttered Robin to himself, *indeed.*

As he approached a work by Anais Nin, more words of wisdom reached his ears.

"We don't see things as they are, we see them as *we* are." *How true,* he agreed, touching the book's spine affectionately.

"Ah, my old friend," said Robin, as he neared a volume by Mark Twain. The former riverboat pilot returned his greeting in the form of one of his favorite lines.

"Good friends, good looks, and a sleepy conscience, this is the ideal life."

"Yes sir," laughed Robin, moving on.

From an upper shelf, came the sound of someone clearing his throat.

"Well, if it's not Mr. George Bernard Shaw, and what do you have to say to inspire my day?"

"Life isn't about finding yourself. Life is about creating yourself." Robin shook his head in full agreement and continued his sojourn through his archive.

At the end of the south wall shelf came the voice of a man he admired beyond most.

"If a cluttered desk is a sign of a cluttered mind, of what, then, is an empty desk a sign?"

Robin gamely parried with, "And if only one side of the desk is cluttered, it must be a sign of a half-wit. Would that not be the case, Mr. Einstein?"

"Great spirits have often encountered violent opposition from weak minds," came his answer.

How fortunate I am to have so many such friends in my house, thought Robin.

* * *

Commencing his stroll along the east wall shelves, he was met by the rhyming of Emily Dickenson.

"They might not need me; but they might. I'll let my head be just in sight; a smile as small as mine might be precisely their necessity."

On the heels of the Amherst poet's final syllable arrived yet another line of winsome verse.

"And, after all, what is a lie? 'Tis but truth in masquerade," declared George Byron, and Robin stopped to ponder the adage.

"Well, your lordship, I suspect a lie *is* a lie regardless of its disguise," he countered.

"Pleasure's a sin, and sometimes sin's a pleasure," retorted Byron. To which Robin replied,

"Not all pleasure is a sin, but I do agree that sometimes we derive pleasure from our sins."

Next, Ernest Hemingway contributed his two cents.

"About morals, I know only that what is moral is what you feel good after and what is immoral is what you feel bad after." Robin nodded in accord and moved along toward a Faulkner tome.

"He has never been known to use a word that might send a reader to the dictionary," observed the bard of Mississippi.

"And one could observe that is where his genius lies," said Robin, in defense of Papa.

Halfway down the row of books, Robin passed a volume by Jane Austen and to his surprise heard nothing at all.

"Why the silence, Jane?" he asked, backing up.

"My sore throats are always worse than anyone's," observed Mr. Darcy's creator. Upon her last hoarse utterance, William Blake chimed in.

"Can I see another's woe, and not be in sorrow too? Can I see another's grief, and not seek for kind relief?" The conversation was beginning to affect Robin's spirits, so he moved away quickly.

Near the north portion of his bibliotheca, Robin encountered Jean-Baptist Poquelin, aka Moliere.

"Of all follies there is none greater than wanting to make the world a better place." Robin shook his head in growing frustration.

"These are not honeyed notions. What is wrong with trying to make the world a better place?" he demurred. To this James Joyce vouchsafed,

"There is no heresy or no philosophy which is so abhorrent to the church as being a human being." Robin sighed deeply and moved with alacrity to the western-most stacks.

* * *

Considering the books before him, he wondered what F. Scott Fitzgerald had to offer.

"In a real dark night of the soul, it is always three o'clock in the morning, day after day." Robin groaned as Dante Alighieri took his turn.

"In the middle of the journey of life I came to myself within a dark wood where the straight way was lost."

"And you, Mr. Lovecraft, what do you have to add to this dismal discourse?" asked Robin with trepidation.

"Bunch together a group of people deliberately chosen to strong feelings, and you have a practical guarantee of dark morbidities expressed in crime, perversion, and insanity."

Thank you for that H.P., grumbled Robin internally, as he shuffled along. His mood had by now reached a new nadir.

He hoped Edith Sitwell would offer a moment's needed light.

"Still falls the rain—dark as the world of man, black as our loss—blind as the nineteen hundred and forty nails upon the cross." Robin whimpered and leaned against the shelf.

"Not you, too, Dame Edith?" He had confused Sitwell for Wharton.

Then a wicked chortle caused his body to stiffen.

"Lucretius, it's you," blurted Robin abjectly.

"Life is one long struggle in the dark," opined the author of the treatise *On the Nature of the Universe,* which stood inches from Robin's nose.

As he headed for the door of his library, he was further assailed by quotes from a bevy of notorious penmen.

"It is better to be feared than loved," declared Niccolo Machiavelli.

"Death is the solution to all problems. No man—no problem," asserted Joseph Stalin.

"The part of me which wanders through my mind and never sees or feels actual objects, but which lives in and moves through my passions and my emotions, experiences this world as a horrible nightmare," added Jack Henry Abbott.

"Quiet!" shouted Robin, continuing, "If you can't say anything nice, don't say anything at all."

He threw open the door to his book repository and ran through it. It was the worst day he could recall in his beloved athenaeum, and he prayed his next visit would end on a better note. The irksome sounds from inside the library faded as Robin went to his reading chair and opened the book he had been reading.

"Have one of those days where you just can't win?" asked Pooh Bear.

In Response to the Brash Young Man

The old man replied:

I was your age twenty minutes ago.

And you will understand what I mean

Twenty minutes from now.

Dan the Man

True success is to labor.
—Robert Louis Stevenson

For five years, Dan Clover had served as the assistant manager of the appliance department at his local Sears. It was not where he hoped he would be in his 34th year. At the very least, he figured he would be the store's general manager, and perhaps even a regional manager. Since graduating from junior college in 1966, he had performed with distinction for the national retailer, but promotions came slowly and prospects for advancement looked bleak.

Dan's biggest fear was that he would not break the pattern of underachievement long established by the males in his family. His father, uncle, and grandfather remained low level workers their entire lives and consequently harbored contempt for those who accomplished greater things or had ambitions to do so. He was not exempt from their animus, which deepened when he received his associate degree from the local community college. The resentful words of his father still echoed in his head and haunted him.

"My son the big shot with his hotsy-totsy diploma. Better than your old man now, huh? Well, let's see what you do with it."

Compounding Dan's angst about his slow career advancement was his friends' rapid climb up the ladder of success. His boyhood chum, Jay Shepherd, had caused a stir with his book, *The Virtues of Deceit: A Phenomenologist's Perspective*. Dan felt at odds with the volume's premise, and Jay was too caught up in exploiting his new-found notoriety—i.e., bedding all the women he could, married or otherwise—to discuss it at any length with his friend. Nonetheless, Jay had achieved a level of renown that was hard to deny, even if his path to the brass ring struck Dan as disingenuous.

Another longtime friend, Leo Johnson, had become a rock music impresario, discovering two local boy bands that climbed the recording charts with a series of hit songs. Dan had hung out at the studio with Leo on a few occasions and took note of the fact that his friend was interested in more than just the business aspects of his young protégés.

What galled Dan the most was the impressive rise of his ex-fiancé, Heidi Bosworth. Since their breakup four years earlier, she had gone from the assistant director of a small art gallery to the curator of the Belton Arts and Crafts Museum. Thinking back on his relationship with Heidi, he understood how the union was doomed from the start. *What high priestess of culture would want to be married to a chain store appliance salesman?* Dan sulked.

* * *

Dan had all but given up thinking he would achieve anything significant in life when an idea occurred to him. It came after watching the old Judy Holiday movie *It Should Happen to You*. In the film, the lead character, desperate for fame, has her name placed on a Manhattan billboard. Not having the money to replicate such a feat, Dan decided on another approach. He would cover the city with a piece of graffiti reading—"Dan the Man." He would do it in his best cursive handwriting employing an array of eye-catching primary colors. When it caught the attention of the media, which he felt confident it would, he would reveal his true identity. While his actions would surely raise the ire of local law enforcement, Dan was willing to incur its wrath in exchange for the notice he would achieve.

Over the coming weekend, Dan purchased several cans of spray paint in the most striking tints he could find. He had decided on his initial targets. The first was an abandoned factory he passed on his way to work. For several years he had watched the site fall into disrepair, and this caused him dismay. It was where his father had worked when Dan was a small boy. Before it crumbled completely, he would put his mark on it, and in doing so bring renewed notice to the disintegrating edifice . . . and to himself.

Dan's next target was a vast plywood fence surrounding a construction site a few blocks from his employer. The large surface faced a rotary giving it great visibility to passing traffic. After that he plied his missive on the rusting railroad bridge a mile from his house. By Sunday evening he had managed to paint "Dan the Man" on a fourth target, and he felt his star begin to rise.

During the coming month, he scrawled his Day-Glo manifesto on another twenty-five surfaces around the city. It was becoming impossible to travel the metropolitan area without encountering Dan's handiwork. He wondered when it would catch the attention of the press and kept his eyes on the television screens next to the washers and dryers in his section of the store.

"Hey, Dan the Man!" rang a voice behind him.

"What . . .!" blurted Dan thinking he'd been found out.

"Whoa, take it easy, buddy!" replied a store associate from furniture. "Just talking about all the 'Dan the Man' graffiti out there. You've seen it, right? Hell, you can't miss it. Guy must be a nut case, huh?"

"Yeah," replied Dan, his heart returning to its normal rhythm.

"Pretty cool that he hasn't been caught yet, though. Stealthy dude. Got to admit that."

Dan redirected the conversation and his fellow employee soon returned to his own work area.

Well, 'Dan the Man,' you're sure being noticed, he thought, happily.

* * *

Over the next two weeks, Dan continued his campaign to adorn the city with his bright scribbles. Only once did he come close to being caught when his ladder fell against a car, causing its theft alarm to go off. He quickly departed the site, leaving several cans of spray paint and the ladder behind. After the close call, he decided to put his project on hold for the time being, expecting his enterprise to inspire notice at any moment . . . and it did.

The noon news on Channel 8 was the first to mention the "Dan the Man" graffiti, reporting that police had found the tools of the perpetrator's trade. The broadcast included interviews with an assortment of people regarding their views of the ubiquitous message. While some felt it was sullying the landscape, most appeared intrigued by it, and one person referred to the graffitist as something of a super-hero intent on brightening the drab spaces of a city that sorely needed it.

The evening news repeated the report with even more interviews expressing approval of the city-wide scrawl.

"I think it livens things up and points out just how run down and neglected a lot of places are around here. Good for 'Dan the Man'," proclaimed one person.

Dan was thrilled by what he heard and decided to reveal his true identity to the media the next day. It was his time to bask in the glow of his achievement, and he couldn't wait.

* * *

The next morning Dan sat in front of the television sipping his coffee and eagerly awaited any additional news about his bold action to draw attention to the city's declining appearance. In the intervening hours since the first public mention of his efforts, he had come to embrace the notion that his Krylon painted scribbles were, indeed, a statement about the sad state of the place he'd grown up in.

To his great surprise, the "Dan the Man" story led the news . . . but with a twist that sent Dan's mood into free fall.

"The person responsible for placing graffiti all over the city has come forward. Dan Coleman, an aspiring songwriter, has confessed to writing 'Dan the Man' on dozens of buildings and structures. He claims he did so as a protest against the decline of urban areas throughout the country. Mr. Coleman was arrested but quickly released from jail after a group sympathetic to his cause raised bail. The 'Dan the Man' behind the colorful graffiti has apparently struck a chord with people sharing his concern. Even a member of the city council . . .."

Dan shut the television off and tossed his empty cup into the sink, shattering it.

"He's a fraud! I'm the *real* 'Dan the Man!'" shouted Dan, dashing from the kitchen to his car determined to expose Coleman's lie and claim the spotlight that was due him.

Dan drove directly to the police station to make a confession and inform them of the imposter who claimed to be him.

"Good morning, sir," said Dan to the officer sitting behind counter. "I'm the legitimate 'Dan the Man,' not that phony who confessed to my graffiti."

"I see," said the officer, casually.

"My name is Dan Clover, and every single 'Dan the Man' out there is my work, and my work alone."

"Well, Mr. Clover, I'm afraid you're the fifth 'Dan the Man' who's made that claim this morning, so why don't you just leave me your phone number, and if we have anything to ask you, we'll be in touch, okay?"

"Fifth!" said Dan, incredulously. "They're all phonies trying to cash in on my work."

"Yeah, I know. That's what they said, too. Now if you'll excuse me, I have other crimes to deal with," replied the officer, turning away from Dan.

* * *

Over the next two days, the news was abuzz about the individual claiming to be the actual 'Dan the Man.' He was portrayed as an activist and hailed for his actions to raise the public's awareness of the city's blighted areas. Incensed by being cheated out of his moment in the spotlight, Dan walked out on his job when the television sets adjacent to his department brought further news of the graffiti interloper.

"Because of the attention 'Dan the Man' has brought to the problem of urban decay, charges have been dropped against him. In fact, the mayor's office has commissioned Dan Coleman to add his iconic graffiti to the scroll of local heroes in the city hall lobby."

Badly upset by the bad luck that had befallen him, Dan experienced insomnia. He tossed and turned while churning thoughts of how fame had been stolen from him. As he lay in bed in the early morning hours of his second sleepless night, an idea occurred to him. He would begin a new campaign designed to discredit the phony "Dan the Man." The following evening he would commence spray painting "The *Real* Dan the Man" across his original graffiti.

With his spirits renewed, Dan purchased the material needed to execute his plan of retaliation. As he anxiously waited nightfall, Dan decided to trace the trajectory of his first campaign. When the time came, he returned to the abandoned building where his father once labored. There he began to scrawl "The *Real* Dan the Man" over his previous art work. Halfway through he was startled by what he took as the gruff voice of his long-departed parent.

"Come down right now before you fall, son!"

The ghostly admonition caused Dan to drop the can of spray paint and freeze where he stood.

"You're under arrest. Now get down before I come up and bring you down."

Dan suddenly realized that it wasn't his deceased dad but a policeman standing at the base of the steps leading up to the wall he had defiled for a second time.

"Now, son! Right now!" barked the officer.

"I'm coming," replied Dan, descending the steps in disbelief that he had been caught on his very first attempt to rectify the injustice against him.

"I was just . . . ." began Dan, as he reached the waiting policeman.

"I'll do the talking," interrupted the officer. "What are you doing up there? Don't you know defiling property is against the law? You're trespassing, too."

"I was trying to . . ." replied Dan, attempting to answer his inquisitor, who again cut him off.

"What's your name, son?"

"Dan Clover. I'm the real . . . ."

"Don't tell me. You're the one who started it all, right? The guy who did the original 'Dan the Man' graffiti. The one that's a big hero now. That who you are . . . *huh?*" asked the officer, sarcastically.

"Well, yes I . . ..":

"Don't give me that bullshit! You're just a pathetic copycat trying to get your fifteen minutes of fame riding the coat tails of the real 'Dan the Man.' There's been a bunch of you creeps claiming to be him. So who are you anyway?"

After a long pause, Dan answered.

"I'm no one . . . *no* one at all."

In the Shadow of Light

Oh, the glory of seeing things not there.
—Anonymous

Lawton Lane was a quiet *cul de sac* consisting of four well-maintained bungalows that led to a small field where a house belonging to the street's namesake had once stood. The early 20th century dwellings inhabited the far reaches of a sleepy hamlet in southeastern Tennessee known for its ore mining. For the most part, the people that lived on Lawton Lane kept to themselves, not venturing beyond their small tracts of land. In fact, they rarely communicated even with their neighbors, except on a very special occasion once a year. To any passerby, the tiny subdivision appeared unexceptional. But to those who lived there, it was anything but that.

On January 15th, in recent years, the street's residents had experienced a series of peculiar visions that happened to coincide with the death of famed humanitarian Howard Rasmus Lawton in a fire that had gutted his mansion. To begin with, regardless of what the weather was beyond Lawton Lane, the sun bathed the short street in radiant light between noon and 1 P.M. If that was not strange enough, at some point during that one-hour span a deep shadow was cast on the treeless lane reaching just beyond the empty Lawton lot.

It was within that dusky veil that people witnessed events that initially frightened but then thrilled them. The occupants of 1, 3, 5, and 7 Lawton Lane saw what at first appeared to be just pieces of random objects but as the years passed they began to take a form that made everyone eager for their future appearances. On this particular January 15th, they believed what they had long awaited would finally come to fruition. The prospect of a visit from a fully evolved (i.e., materialized) circus filled them with great excitement. No longer would just the bulbous noses of clowns, pearly tusks of elephants, decorated rumps of prancing horses, rings and balls of jugglers, and snapping whips of animal trainers be discernable.

When the special day arrived everyone kept a close watch on the sky, and during the midday period when previous sightings had occurred, a shadow again spread over the street as if choreographed by the sun itself.

Calliope music, which until now had only been heard in snippets, grew louder as a full-fledged big top parade began to reveal itself to Lawton Lane's waiting spectators.

"It's here! It's *all* here!" shouted a rotund woman in a beige smock standing in front of the street's first dwelling, and others down the lane echoed her words.

Led by a sequined baton twirler and a red-tuxedo-clad ringmaster, with black stovepipe hat, the parade passed the excited bystanders, and as it did, everyone clapped and cheered with wild delight and then fell in behind it, merrily stepping to the loud rhythms of the clavier.

At the moment the gala procession reached the former Lawton mansion site, a large tent emerged from the barren soil, along with the concession stands and game booths that typically accompany a circus. Lawton Lane's inhabitants sang as they danced up and down the fairway. It was the happiest they had been in memory.

"Stop! Stop! Return to your residences," bellowed two approaching men in uniforms, but the gleeful crowd continued its joyous romp.

"All right, let's get them in their units, John," ordered the elder of the duo.

Within minutes they had corralled everyone and directed the rapturous throng to their designated houses.

"What the hell were they saying about a circus in that empty field?" asked the younger man adjusting the nameplate on his white jacket.

"Mass hysteria is my guess. Not uncommon in this section. This bunch gets nuttier at this time every year for some reason. We'll report it to the shrinks," replied his cohort.

The two men closed and locked the gate at the head of the street and returned to a nearby building marked "Lawton Mental Care Facility." Meanwhile, the asylum's patients watched intently as the traveling show rose to the sky and the shadow that accompanied it give way to the remaining sunlight. They waved a melancholy farewell to the performers and animal trainers, but they were not distraught. They knew an even grander circus would return next year.

Following Heather

And they were gone: aye, ages long ago
These lovers fled away into the storm.
—John Keats

It was not possible that she was dead . . . it could not be true, the horrible thought ripped Cary from a fitful sleep. *Oh, God, but it was . . . it was true!* He leapt to his feet to catch the air suddenly drawn from his lungs. *She was alive in this room yesterday morning*, he recalled, as dawn peeked from behind the drawn curtains. Cary caught the scent of his wife's perfume and thought she was there with him . . . still under the covers. He turned hopefully, but the bed was empty—barren like his soul. *He couldn't make it without her*, he thought, tears drenching the collar of his nightshirt. He didn't want to. She was his life partner, and he couldn't imagine living without her.

In the months following Heather's funeral, Cary attempted to return to his former existence, but he had little zeal and even less focus. He slowly went back to work and resumed construction on a backyard storage shed. He did his best to appear normal to friends and neighbors all the while dying by inches inside. In the evenings, he would drink himself numb and cry himself to sleep. Within moments of the alarm clock sounding, despair reclaimed him, and he had to muster the limited will in him simply to deal with the day ahead. It took everything he had to keep his grief from over-powering him. People told him it would get better, but he doubted their words. What he felt was too huge to overcome. It had permeated his being and would not disappear by just waiting it out.

* * *

Meg and Bob Silva, the couple Cary and Heather had long been closest to, lived just a block away and made frequent attempts to bring him around and lighten his burden. It soon became clear that their good intentions and formidable efforts were not up to the challenge.

"He's a Fort Knox of angst," observed Meg Silva to her husband after they had made an unannounced visit to Cary's house.

"I knew they had a great marriage, but I didn't realize they were so dependent on each other," responded Bob.

"I did," said Meg. "She was crazy in love with him, and she knew he was with her. I can't believe she's gone. I never knew cancer could get you that fast. She was fine a month before she died. Lost a little weight, but I actually thought she was watching her diet. It's just incredible."

"I'm really worried about Cary. Nothing seems to give him lift off. Just remains in his dark space," observed Bob.

Cary had declined several invitations from Bob to do things, but what really got his attention was when Cary refused to accompany him to the Philly's opener. They had not missed the season's first game in ten years.

"He just needs a change. Maybe get out of that house of theirs. He should sell the place. Get a condo where he could start over and meet new people . . . women."

"Jeez, Bob, give him time. Heather's only been gone a few months."

"I know. I'm not saying he should start dating, but he needs some distraction." After a pause, Bob added, "He should go storm chasing. Remember when he brought that up when we were with him and Heather? She kind of freaked. Read him the riot act. Told him she'd never let him do it."

"I do remember. He was serious. Said it was something he always wanted to do. Heather had a bird though when he mentioned it. I don't blame her. That's a crazy thing."

"It's not *that* dangerous. You go with a group led by professionals. They don't take risks with customers. They give you a nice box lunch and take you within miles of a twister. You get great pictures and bragging rights. I wouldn't mind doing it myself," said Bob, testing Meg's reaction.

"Not on my watch, sweetie," replied Meg. "You go chasing storms, you'll find a perfect storm waiting for you when you get back."

"Just kidding, honey," replied Bob, sheepishly.

"Maybe you should encourage Cary to go," suggested Meg. "Something crazy and consuming like that might be just what he needs."

"I'll go over tomorrow and plant the seed. Not sure anything will appeal to him at this point though. You saw how he is. Talk about hurting. The pain has deep roots."

* * *

To Bob's surprise his suggestion was not greeted with total indifference. In fact, it was the first time since Heather's untimely death that Carl's gloom lifted, if only for a moment.

"It's a thought. I don't know though. I got work, and I'm not finished with the shed," replied Carl.

"You need a break, and storm chasing has always been something you wanted to do. So you should go for it now that you can," said Bob, regretting his last words. "I mean, you have the time, right . . . *shit!* I'm sorry. Nothing's coming out right."

"Don't worry about it, Bob. Hey, if you don't mind, I've got a few things to do, so . . . ."

"Sure," said Bob, moving to the door. I have some errands I have to take care of, too. Think about the storm chasing. Wish I could go, but you know, Meg's not hot on the idea. Like Heather . . . ah, *damn* . . . well, okay. Take care, buddy."

Cary watched from a window as Bob walked away shaking his head in obvious displeasure over his inept comments. When he was out of sight, Cary went to his desk and withdrew a pamphlet from Twister Tours he had sent away for a year earlier when he had broached the topic with Heather.

"Sorry baby," whispered Bob, glancing at her framed photo. "I've really got to do this. It'll be all right. You'll see."

His eyes returned to the page before him and his expression hardened.

"But not for five grand!" he uttered, chucking the brochure back into the desk drawer.

The more Cary considered heading to tornado country, the more he embraced the idea as the possible remedy to his current state of mind. Few things had fascinated him more than monster twisters. They had intrigued him since childhood. He regarded their awesome destructive power as the hammer of God, and it was that hammer he wished to experience now that his beloved spouse was gone.

* * *

It took Cary less than a month to fully commit to the idea, and as fate would have it his timing was perfect. It was May, the height of tornado season. There was no better time for a storm chaser to head to central Oklahoma—the epicenter for twisters. Rather than pay the exorbitant fee charged by companies specializing in that form of adventure tourism, Cary decided to go it alone, a fact he did not reveal when he told the Silvas of his plans.

"You'll have fun. Something you can use a bunch of," said Meg, adding, "Just don't let them get you too close to those things."

"Those companies know what they're doing, honey. They take kids and old people out there to see tornados, but they don't get within miles of them. It's bad for business if your customers get killed," offered Bob, winking at Cary.

"I'll be fine, guys. Appreciate you keeping an eye on my house while I'm away. Be back on the eighteenth. You have my cell number. Sure you don't want to come along?" joked Cary.

"No, that's okay. You know what they say, one person's heaven is another person's hell," cracked Meg.

"Maybe another time," said Bob, glancing at his wife longingly. "Have a great time, buddy, and don't let the wind blow up your knickers. Send pictures when you spot the big one, but use a telephoto lens."

* * *

The drive out from New Jersey to Oklahoma took Cary a couple of days. He settled on a tiny town called Drummond as a destination, since he'd heard it had been the location of several recent tornado sightings. Cary rented a room at the town's only motel and for the next few days monitored the atmospheric conditions on a weather radio he had purchased at a Radio Shack before setting out on his expedition. He tuned the pocket size receiver to the NOAA Weather Alert Emergency Channel and listened patiently while cruising the flat countryside of north central Oklahoma. On his first day out, he encountered a storm chaser van and followed it for several hours without incident, despite intense weather activity under threatening skies.

After awhile, the sparse landscape began to get to him. The loneliness he'd experienced back home returned with the same horrible intensity. He pulled off the road and wept as clouds accumulated on the far horizon.

"Heather," he moaned over and over until emotional exhaustion overtook him.

An hour after he dozed off, a strident tone from his weather radio awakened him. The day was no longer bright. The scene beyond his windshield had turned darkly ominous. Less than a mile down the road was a massive funnel cloud scattering everything in its path.

"Yes," muttered Cary, moving the car back onto the road.

As the tornado moved closer, Cary sped toward it.

"Heather!" he cried out, and then the swirling column of savage air lifted him into her arms.

Tele/kinetic

*Blind fortune still bestows her gifts
on such as cannot use them.*
—Ben Johnson

It happened while Susan Collier was watching *Fat Loss*. The words in her head became those of the popular television show's leading contestant.

"I want a Twinkie!" blurted a large male in sweatpants in answer to the host's question about what he hoped for in life now that he had lost over one hundred pounds.

It was not the answer the host expected.

So do I, thought Susan, amused that both she and the show's star contestant would be thinking of the same thing.

When she returned from the kitchen with a package of Twinkies and a glass of milk, the host of *Fat Loss* was interviewing another weight reduction competitor.

"So what's it like being on *Fat Loss* and shedding 75 pounds?"

It's not that great, thought Susan, as she took her first bite of the Twinkie.

"It's not that great," replied the contestant, to the show's perplexed emcee.

"Huh?" muttered Susan, thinking she'd heard her thought mimicked by the television. *How crazy is that,* she contemplated, putting aside the disappointing snack.

"Crazy?" asked the television host, and Susan starred at the screen in astonishment.

Could it be repeating my thought? she wondered, deciding to test the bizarre possibility. Again she looked intensely at the television screen—focusing on the female contestant—and formulated a sentence in her mind.

"You're a hot looking guy," said the game show contender to her startled host, Lyle Connor.

Oh my god! Whoever I look at on the TV says what I'm thinking, concluded Susan in total disbelief.

Susan hit the off switch on the remote to further consider the astonishing revelation without distraction. *How can I do that?* she wondered, but then her thoughts turned to other things. *What would she do with the newfound ability? Was it something she could use to her benefit?* If nothing else, she could have some fun, she figured, and then questioned whether it was only the content on her *own* television that she could alter.

Susan got her answer the next morning at work at the Coyne Elder Care Facility when a fellow nurse's aid and good friend, Sally Morse, remarked about the strange comments by the contestants on *Fat Loss*.

"This guy on the show said he wanted a Twinkie and this chick came on to the host. It was hysterical."

"Really?" replied Susan, saying nothing about her possible role in the spectacle.

"Lyle Connor looked like a deer in the headlights. Didn't know how to respond. Like, what do you say to a guy on *Fat Loss* asking for a Twinkie? I almost peed my pants. Lyle probably crapped his. It was *sooo* funny," recounted Sally, chuckling.

So it really happened, mulled Susan, experiencing both excitement and a twinge of apprehension.

* * *

When Susan returned home after work and grocery shopping, she was eager to see if she still had the power to alter the words of television personalities. During the course of the day, she had considered many possibilities of what she might do with her miraculous skill . . . if she still possessed it.

She quickly stored her groceries and nuked an enchilada for supper. When it was ready, she took it along to the living room with a glass of white wine and pressed the power button on the television remote. Her favorite program, *Rough Love*, was about to start, and Susan planned to toy with the dialogue of the program's most detested character, Price Everlowe. For several years Susan had witnessed Everlowe ruin the lives of people she loved on the show, and if she could get him to say things contrary to his hateful nature, it would give her tremendous satisfaction.

As soon as Everlowe appeared on the screen, Susan began manipulating his speech. Finding, indeed, that her strange ability was still very much intact.

I would like to apologize to everyone for all of the pain and heartbreak I've caused over the years, thought Susan, and Price Everlowe repeated her words verbatim.

This caused the other actors to look at him strangely, although they continued with their dialogue as if Everlowe had remained in character.

"Why must you treat me like a common street urchin instead of your child?" asked a young actress forging ahead with her part in the melodrama.

"I am eternally sorry for behaving so cruelly to you, my dearest daughter," replied Everlowe, whose words belied his malevolent expression.

Susan could not contain her delight and laughed loudly as she continued to apply her odd powers.

By the end of *Rough Love*, she had managed to reduce its foremost antagonist to that of a pathetic whiner. Tickled with her handiwork, Susan called her friend to get her reaction to the show.

"Do you think they're trying to kill off Everlowe? Why would they change him so much? I liked him better when he was a bastard," responded Sally.

Again, Susan felt exhilaration knowing that she could alter television's content.

"I did it," blurted Susan, impulsively, immediately regretting her words.

"You did what?' asked Sally.

"Nothing," replied Susan.

"Come on, you did what?" pressed Sally.

"Well . . . I think I can make people say things on television," admitted Susan, reluctantly.

"What do you mean?"

"You know how the people on *Fat Loss* acted weird the other day?" asked Susan.

"Yeah, that was really funny," responded Sally with a giggle. "You're not saying you did that, are you?"

"I think so. I mean, yes. I did that," asserted Susan.

After a short silence, Sally spoke, "That's crazy. How could you do that? Are you joking?"

"No, I'm not joking. Come over and I'll show you," answered Susan.

"I'll be right there!" shouted Sally into her cellphone, and within twenty minutes she was at Susan's door.

* * *

For the balance of the evening, Susan demonstrated her wizardry to the complete amazement of her friend.

"Wow, this is outrageous. You could do other things, you know. What about if you made the lottery host call your numbers?" inquired Sally, excitedly.

"I can't change what you see, only what you hear. The numbers would be there, so whatever he said, you could still see the actual winning figures," replied Susan.

"Well, there must be something," said Sally, getting up to leave.

"Don't tell anybody about this, okay?" pleaded Susan.

"Why not? This can make you famous," replied Sally, surprised at her friend's modesty.

"It would make me a freak, more than anything. And it will probably go away. Could be just a temporary thing. Then where would I be?"

"Well, think about it anyway, and I won't tell a soul . . . I promise. See you tomorrow at work," said Sally, exiting her friend's apartment.

Susan found it difficult to get to sleep. She wondered if she'd done the right thing revealing her peculiar talent to Sally. She also pondered what she could do with her gift that would have a positive effect. *She might be able to do something good . . . but what?* Susan contemplated. It was nearly sunrise when she finally fell asleep. But by that time she had devised a plan that might help change the world . . . or so she hoped.

* * *

The next evening, Susan awaited the State of the Union Address by the President—a broadcast she seldom, if ever, watched. It had been a long day at work, made more protracted by her eagerness to implement her idea. Susan was also concerned by the seeming aloofness of Sally, who barely spoke to her other than to tell her that the news was filled with reports of what she had done to last night's television shows. Because of her friend's apparent coolness, she decided against confiding her intentions to alter the speech of the nation's leader.

What was behind Susan's plan was her anger at the President for his recent commitment of thousands of troops to several countries. His decisions had resulted in global condemnation and a growing casualty count among soldiers and innocent civilians. While Susan didn't care much about politics, she was worried about the country's ever-growing military involvement in the affairs of nearly a dozen foreign nations while at home the U.S. economy continued to falter. She knew too many people who were suffering the consequences of her country's bad decisions, and it disturbed her.

Susan settled into her chair as an announcer introduced the President. Not long into his address, she began to put words into his mouth.

"For too long we have sent our soldiers and resources to far-off lands while the national debt has climbed and unemployment has soared. It costs billions of taxpayers' dollars to send our military to places where we have no business being. This unnecessary expense has contributed to the continuing deterioration of our nation's roads, highways, and historical structures, as well as the loss of programs designed to provide humanitarian assistant to disadvantaged citizens. Our lust for war and global dominance has nearly destroyed this once great nation . . ."

The furor over the President's speech raged for days but received kudos from the international community. The headlines in *Le Monde, Pravda, El Mundo, The Guardian, Deutsche Welle,* and *Times of India*, to name just a few, expressed both surprise and delight, commending the U.S. President for the radical shift in his foreign policy strategy. While his critics appeared mystified though at the same time pleased with his sudden change of heart, his own supporters and party leaders were confounded. The President himself was aghast by what had occurred during his national address.

"I must have had some sort of spasm or something," he speculated to his staff and the heads of his now-shaky political alliance.

Given the favorable response from the global community, the President's people were at a loss as to what to do next. They feared a conspiracy by the liberal media but were not inclined to go public with the assertion, because they had heard the networks had experienced similar disruptions with other broadcasts, though not of a political nature.

* * *

When Sally returned from a visit with her mother in Wheeling, she had lunch with Susan at work.

"I can't believe what you did to the President," whispered Sally, excitedly. "They could get you good for that. Isn't it treason or something like that? I mean, messing with the President's speech . . . *oh, my god!*"

"I wanted to do something worthwhile with my . . . my gift. I hate to see all those innocent people killed in the wars. All that money spent on destruction when people here at home don't have jobs and are losing their homes."

"That's really nice. Will you do something for me?" asked Sally, moving closer to Susan. "Will you get me on *Ellen*?"

"What?" replied Susan,

"You know, *The Ellen Degeneres Show*. I love her. I want to be on her show so bad, and you can do it. Just make her invite me, and then she'll have to let me on," pleaded Sally.

"I can't," answered Susan, moving away from Sally, who was practically in her lap.

"Why not? It's not a big thing that I'm asking. I mean, not like changing the President's address," retorted Sally.

"I don't feel right about doing it. I know I did some things before, but I'm just going to try to do some good with my ability . . . while it lasts."

"Well, you'd be doing *me* some good . . . like, hello, I'm your *friend* sitting here," protested Sally, stiffening in her seat.

"I'm sorry. I just don't think it's right. This power was given to me for a purpose, and I should use it in a positive way."

"Oh, and doing something for *me* wouldn't be a positive thing?" said Sally, perturbed.

"You know what I mean, Sally. Please don't be mad," begged Susan, but Sally stood up and stormed away.

* * *

Susan heard nothing from Sally for several days. She had not even appeared at work nor did she return her phone calls. At that point, Susan feared her friend had reported her to the authorities. Nonetheless, she was committed to her plan to use her powers for peaceful purposes. To her satisfaction, she quickly got another opportunity when the President's staff decided to throw caution to the winds and scheduled a televised news conference to allow him to clarify the statements he made during his ill-fated State of the Union Address.

"Good evening, my fellow citizens," greeted the President, as Susan leaned toward the television screen and began projecting words into his mouth.

"I wish to restate my determination to create peace in the world through the reduction of our military forces and our involvement in the politics of other nations. No longer will our soldiers take up arms against foreign lands. America will mind its business and focus its attention exclusively on its own challenges and problems. The government will treat its citizens with the fairness and openness they deserve. You have my wor . . .."

At that exact moment, the broadcast from the White House ceased and Susan slumped lifelessly to the floor. She never heard the shot. Beyond the shattered pane in her apartment window, a camouflaged figure scurried away.

Years

*He more rightly deserves the name of happy
who knows how to use the gifts wisely.*
—Horace

When he was a child, aliens had entered Vince Abbott's life. The encounters were not infrequent, coming about a month apart over a period of a year. The first time he was abducted, at seven years old, he felt more curiosity than fear. It seemed like an odd dream involving cartoon-like creatures with huge luminous eyes and warm smiles. They had done nothing to arouse his anxiety or cause him discomfort. Little Vinny, as his parents lovingly called him, had been gently removed from his house and taken to a white, windowless room. There he was placed on a soft table the shape of the mushrooms his grandmother picked on the hill above her house. During his captivities—as the strange creatures touched him without seeming to touch him—he heard sounds that reminded him of the melodic chirping outside his bedroom window at sunrise.

The several encounters that followed left him with no immediate memories. In fact, two decades would pass before Vince would begin to recall the long-ago nocturnal visits. At first the recollections trickled in and began to spook him. He feared he was losing his mind and wasn't sure what to do. He thought about seeking a professional explanation before telling his wife, who was suffering the effects of the difficult delivery of their first child. In the end, he chose to hold off on both counts because of a growing sense that he had been given something important, even precious, by the extraterrestrials. What it was, however, remained beyond his grasp. Until late one night . . ..

On his way to his daughter's room in response to her cries, the answer hit him like an unexpected thunderclap. *One hundred years*, thought Vince, *they gave me a century of life to use as I see fit.* His sketchy memory of the aliens' farewell gesture began to crystalize, and now he knew that it had been their way of offering recompense for whatever it was they derived from their transactions with him. Their gift of time was payback for services rendered. Thankfully, he bore no physical evidence of their explorations.

I can live a hundred years beyond my normal lifespan, he reflected, amazed and excited by the prospect. *I'd be the oldest person in history! Maybe one hundred eighty years old or more.* Being famous for being old was not something Vince fantasized, but fame was fame, and the idea intrigued him.

* * *

Vince told no one about his extraordinary revelation believing such an admission would be met with skepticism, if not ridicule. *What's the matter with you? You've really lost it,* he imagined everyone saying, including his wife, Michele. As the days passed, the idea of using the remarkable largesse just for his own benefit struck him as selfish, and he decided to share the bequest with his loved ones. He would extend the lives of his wife, mother—unfortunately his father had recently died—sister, uncle, and best friend. Since his baby daughter had her full life ahead of her, Vince felt he did not need to invest her with additional years. The actuarial tables had her living to be one hundred anyway. Time was on her side.

He knew that by touching those he wished to endow with surplus years and silently repeating the amount of time he chose to give them it would result in the transfer. Somehow that knowledge had been programmed into him too. After considerable thought, he decided to keep forty years for himself, giving his wife twenty years (reasoning that women normally lived longer) and the others a decade each. Vince wondered if the aging process would cease when they entered the extra years or whether they would continue to show the effects of time. *God, what would I look like at 120 years old?* he mulled, with a shudder.

In short order Vince had extended the lives of those he had chosen. One by one, he altered the trajectory of their existences. *I give you twenty years, Michele. I give you ten years, Mother . . ..* He wished he could tell them how lucky they were, *but how would they react to the news,* he mused? It pained him that he could not let them know without their thinking he had gone over the edge. *You did what? Extended our lives? What, with your magic wand?*

If he did let the cat out of the bag, he would then have to reveal his childhood encounters with the aliens, and that would be the clincher. He'd be rushed to the loony bin. Five years into his career as a cop would be jeopardized if word got out. The law enforcement profession was not known for its compassion when it came to employing the mentally ill, and that is how he would be classified. *So you were abducted by little green men? Well, isn't that nice. Your final check will be mailed to you, Officer Abbott.*

No, he would have to keep quiet about it and derive satisfaction from the knowledge he had done something wonderful for those he loved. That would have to be enough, yet the thought of not revealing his magnanimity gnawed at him. It took awhile, but eventually Vince accepted the situation for what it was. He derived solace from the fact that those he most cared for in the world would live longer because of him. Ultimately the thought made his life sweeter. Unlike the rest of humankind, Vince and his kin would not suffer the usual effects of heredity and happenstance, at least not for many years.

* * *

All in all, life was good for Vince . . . until it took a sudden dark turn. A week after the Abbotts' daughter Nina's second birthday, the toddler took sick. Less than a month later she was diagnosed with a rare form of lymphoma and given a limited time to live. Vince and Michele were beside themselves with grief. They spent endless hours desperately searching the Internet for information about the disease, hoping to come across some experimental treatment that might extend their child's life. However, their formidable effort went unrewarded. No remedy existed that would reverse or even forestall her death sentence.

As Nina's condition began to deteriorate, the Abbotts were told the child would have to spend her remaining time in the hospital.

"We can make her comfortable. She won't suffer," promised the oncologist.

"I don't want her to suffer," said Michele, as if not hearing what the doctor had just said.

"She won't suffer," he repeated.

"Little children should never suffer."

"We do our best to prevent that," assured the doctor, wanly. "We'll see you on the fifteenth. Let me know if anything changes with Nina before then."

"We will," replied Vince, escorting his distraught wife from the doctor's office.

Since his daughter's diagnosis, regret about not extending her life as he had the others plagued Vince. *If I had just given her a few years, it may have made a difference. A cure may have been found in that time,* he obsessed. As the date to take her to the hospital approached, his regret turned to deep guilt and self-loathing. *How could I have been such a thoughtless parent,* he lamented, as he lay awake night after night.

It was during this sleepless period that Vince wondered if he could make contact with his former abductors. If he could, he would beg them to let him reassign his years to his dying daughter. If reconnection with the aliens was at all possible, he figured he would need to be alone. Thus he used his insomnia as an excuse to move to the guest room. He encountered no resistance from his wife, who had become nearly mute in her grief. It was obvious she wasn't getting any sleep either, because he had seen her staring at the ceiling at all hours of the night.

Vince lay awake in the guest bed for several hours and near dawn finally drifted off. In a light dream state, he sensed the presence of the aliens. He was not, as in the encounters of his childhood, removed to a windowless room and placed on a mushroom-shaped table. Nor did he see the creatures that had hovered over him on those occasions. Nonetheless, he felt they were there, and he made a desperate plea to let him give his years to his dying daughter.

Not long after, he awoke with a vague feeling that something significant had happened and slowly recalled that night's experience. Uncertain whether he had actually encountered his abductors, Vince nonetheless ran to his daughter's room to make the time transfer.

As he gently caressed his sleeping child, he repeated the words, "I give you my years. I give you all my years." Almost immediately, he felt intense fatigue, as if the incantation had drained him of all of his energy. It took a huge effort for Vince to return to the guest room bed, where he slipped under the covers and immediately fell into a deep slumber.

* * *

Michele Abbott watched as the sun rose over the distant hills. She had passed another night steeped in her measureless grief.

"Please, God, don't let this happen," she mumbled repeatedly, as she put on her robe and headed to her daughter's room. As soon as she opened the door, Michele knew her prayers had been answered. Nina was standing on her bed with her arms outstretched in greeting to her mother. All the color that had left her face in recent weeks had returned, as had the sparkle in her large eyes.

"Mommy... Mommy, let's play!" she shouted joyfully, leaping to the floor and running to her mother's side.

"My darling, you're better. So much better," cried Michele, ecstatically grateful for her child's miraculous transformation.

"Can I have some ice cream?" asked Nina, with a wide smile.

"You can have anything you want, sweetheart, but first let's show daddy how happy we are."

Michele took her daughter's hand and they went to the guest room.

"Vince! Vince!" she shouted, gleefully, opening the guest bedroom door. "Honey, we have our daughter back. Look . . . she's completely recovered."

Michele pulled the covers off her husband and let out a scream. Before her lay a withered old man, whose half-open eyes gazed out at eternity.

On a Cold Damp April Night

Tinsel reflect

Electrical speck

Glossy pink shadow

Titanic bulk wreck

Scar

There is no trusting appearances.
—Richard Brinsley Sheridan

When she was six years old, Mary Corkum fell face first into broken glass while roller-skating. The accident left jagged scars—one-inch ravines—in her left and right cheeks that caused her endless embarrassment and shame. The adhesions diminished her self-regard, and even the esteem her family held for her. She had been a beautiful child, possessing everything most cherished in someone of her tender years—radiant complexion, curly golden locks, and eyes the color of polished tanzanite. Mary had been the center of her parents' universe until shards from a discarded bottle ruined her beauty. The Corkums were never able to look at their daughter the same way again; some of the adoration had left their gaze.

Although they continued to love Mary, it was not with the same intensity as when she appeared perfect to them. In their minds, something precious had been lost, and their disappointment was palpable to little Mary. She knew before her stitches were removed that they loved her less. This pained her and began to maim her soul. The bedtime lullaby her mother sang lacked its former honey tones. It was flat . . . compulsory. Her father did his best to avoid looking at her at all. His once deep loving stares were replaced by elusive glances. It was as if he dreaded fixing his gaze on her damaged face.

Things were even worse outside her home. In grade school, her facial lesions led to the terrible teasing and hurtful comments that children can so easily make. Her classmates regarded her disfigured face with a mixture of fascination and disgust. She was mocked with hurtful nicknames. One, in particular, stuck like a leech.

"'Hey, *Boris*, how'd you get so ugly?' 'Here comes *Boris*, the monster girl,' 'Are you gonna' kill us, *Boris* face?'" taunted the boys, while the girls would just crinkle their noses and giggle when they saw her.

Mary had heard them whisper the disparaging epithet many times, and she felt both angry and hurt. From the first grade onward, she began distancing herself from everyone, including her teachers, whom she believed also behaved as if she were different. Having heard the boys call her Boris, one substitute teacher asked her how she came by that odd name, and when Mary just glowered at her, the young woman realized her mistake and quickly changed the subject.

In the schoolyard and in the cafeteria, she kept away from her peers, which only made her seem all the more peculiar. On two occasions, a girl in her grade attempted to befriend her, but Mary was suspicious of her overtures and rejected her well-meaning efforts. She preferred to spare herself any further indignities that seemed to come from any contact with others. *People were just cruel*, she thought, and so she decided to have little to do with humans, contenting herself by drawing disparaging caricatures of those around her. The boys that called her names were drawn with crooked smiles, horns, and bulbous noses and ears, while the girls were given spindly torsos, giant feet, and ghastly hairdos. Disfiguring them with her color pencils made her feel less disfigured—less homely. It was her way of getting even for the callousness she was subjected to every day.

At home Mary would sketch for hours to try to limit the hurt stemming from the ridicule and scorn. As the years passed, Mary's skill as an artist grew as did the hideousness of the subjects she drew. She kept her work to herself, except for a few floral landscapes that she painted to justify to her parents the long stretches of time she spent alone in her room. They took little interest in Mary's activities and that came to suit her. The satisfaction she got from corrupting the flesh of her antagonists filled the void.

* * *

One day an unexpected knock on her door sent her scrambling to hide her drawings.

"We have wonderful news, Mary. You are going to have a baby sister," announced her parents, gleefully. "How about that. Isn't that great? Are you happy?"

Mary feigned delight, but in her heart felt little joy. When the baby was born, she remained unmoved, but as her mother and father poured all of their affection into the infant, her indifference turned to jealousy. As time passed, Mary grew more invisible to her parents, who devoted themselves entirely to the toddler.

One particular comment by her mother cut Mary to the core and filled her with despair and then rage.

"She looks just like you used to, Mary. She's so beautiful."

Mary ran to her room and wept. She then began to draw her family as abominably as she had the kids at school that derided her. She worked hard to capture her parents' likenesses, and when she achieved the desired result, sat on her bed looking at them for a very long time.

Why had they forsaken her because of the scars on her face? she wondered. *How could they stop loving her because of the accident?*

Her sorrow was replaced by ire. *If they could treat her with so little regard because of her tragic mishap, they were bad parents and they deserved to be punished*, she concluded.

On each of their faces, she painted scars far exceeding the severity of her own.

"This is what you look like to me!" she repeated over and over again, fury mounting in her voice.

With the intended effect achieved, Mary felt her anger subside. She then painted her baby sister with the intention of scarring her face the way she had her parents, but when the time came to do so, she found she could not. Only then did she realize that she, too, loved the little girl.

Along with that epiphany came a loud scream from the living room. She pressed her ear to her bedroom door to determine its cause. Mary's parents were clearly deeply upset about something.

"Look at me! It's horrible! Oh, my God! It's worse than Mary's," cried her mother.

"Me, too," replied her husband, aghast.

Mary turned to the paintings of her parents and wondered if what she had done to their faces on canvas had actually come to pass. She crept to where her parents were and peeked in at them as they sat on the front room couch solemnly staring at each other as they wept. Indeed, their faces were marred with ugly scars just like those she had added to their portraits.

Mary felt elation rather than remorse. *Now they would experience the cruelty she had.* When she returned to her room and closed the door to block her parents' sobs, an idea occurred to her. *If she painted herself without the scars, would they disappear?*

* * *

In less than an hour, she had a good likeness of herself... sans scars. When she looked at her face in her only mirror, hidden in the bottom drawer of her dresser, her heart skipped. Her scars were gone. It was as if she were seeing her true self for the first time. *I am pretty*, she thought, fighting back tears.

Mary heard her sibling crying in her room across the hall. She had been doing so for some time, which was very unusual. Her parents never allowed the child to cry longer than it took for one of them to reach her. Mary went to her sister and soothed her.

"It's all right. I'm here," she said, caressing the toddler's tear drenched cheeks.

Mary could hear her parent's abject moans as she lay beside her sister, and for the first time she felt as content as she had before the broken glass had torn her life apart.

"We're perfect," she whispered into her baby sister's ear. "*Totally* perfect."

A Better Life

I have, alas, only one illusion left.
—Sydney Smith

It was the last thing he was in the mood to hear as he finished his morning coffee before embarking on his dreaded daily grind.

"Can you pick up some half-and-half on your way home?"

Seymour Bauls' retired brother and housemate, Gil, sat across from him at the kitchen table in his soiled t-shirt and boxers, crumbs from a piece of toast stuck to his upper lip.

Why can't you do it? You're going to be home all day, for Chris sakes, thought Seymour, disgustedly.

"Yeah, yeah, I'll get it," he conceded, grabbing his briefcase and heading for the door.

"See you tonight," mumbled Seymour's elder sibling.

Gil Bauls would spend the rest of the morning in the kitchen reading the newspaper before shifting his base of inactivity to the living room to watch game shows.

"Sure, whatever," responded Seymour, shutting the door behind him and heading to his car in the driveway.

What a piece of shit, he reflected, taking in the length of his dilapidated 14-

year-old Escort.

Not surprisingly it took him a couple of tries to get its engine to turn over, and as usual the highway into the city was clogged with traffic, inflaming Seymour.

"Goddamn it!" he shouted, pounding the steering wheel and giving drivers in adjacent lanes dirty looks.

Long commutes invariably raised his blood pressure, which was already a problem requiring daily medication. Despite giving himself more than enough time to reach his workplace, he was fifteen minutes late. In a fitful mood, he ignored the greetings of colleagues and went directly to his small office in the tax and accounting firm. Closing the door, he sequestered himself until lunch.

* * *

"Well, hello, Mr. Grumpy," said Mark Hiller, the closest thing he had to a friend at Boyle Tax Services. "You sure were in a funk this morning, pal. Another miserable drive in, I gather?"

In the warm weather, Seymour typically ate his bag lunch at the picnic table in the so-called green space provided by the firm. He could escape the frigid air of the office for the warmth of the desert sun, relishing the seldom-occupied refuge.

"What are you doing out here, Mark? Why aren't you at the Pig Trough?" asked Seymour, snidely referring to the local 'all you can eat' buffet restaurant nearby.

"Saw you come out, so I thought I'd say hi before heading over. You want to chuck that PB&J and join the rest of us for a change . . . like an adult?"

"Baloney," replied Seymour.

"Ugh," grimaced Mark.

"Bye, Mark," said Seymour, waving him off like he would a fly.

"Wait a minute. My wife knows this gal who's unattached. She's not bad either. Maybe a little on the chubby side, but who isn't? Why don't you come by Saturday, and we can hook you up."

"No thanks. Not interested," said Seymour, biting into his sandwich. "Never any luck in that department. I gave it a good try. Women always hide something from you, and then when they've got you, they reveal their true nature. I'm done being disappointed."

"Jesus, fella. You aren't dead yet. How long has it been since you've been with somebody . . . a woman, I mean?"

"Not long enough," responded Seymour, pieces of chewed baloney falling from his mouth.

"You got to get out . . . your brother, too. At least he had a wife. It's not normal to be single all your life. Think you'd want to give your calloused palm a break."

"Up yours," muttered Seymour.

"Well, think about Saturday night," said Mark, looking at his watch. "Shit, I got to get to Old Country Buffet before they eat up all the honey-barbequed chicken wings. You know how those guys are."

"You mean the Gout Brigade?" said Seymour, sarcastically.

Mark dashed off in the direction of the waiting buffet, while Seymour consumed the remains of his lunch in the restored silence. On his way back into the excessively air conditioned office building, he experienced sudden dizziness, accompanied by a sharp pain behind his eyes.

"You okay, Seymour?" asked Vera, the receptionist.

"Sure . . . think I just ate some bad baloney," replied Seymour, weaving his way down the hall to his office.

"There's no such thing as *good* baloney," shouted the receptionist after him.

By the time Seymour reached his desk his equilibrium had returned and the pain in his head was mostly gone.

Maybe it was *the baloney*, considered Seymour, digging into the pile of papers before him. For the balance of the day, he endured a dull headache, which four Tylenol failed to alleviate. On his way home after work his cellphone rang, and it was his brother again reminding him to pick up cream. It really perturbed Seymour that it had not occurred to Gil to get off his rump and perform the simple errand himself. After all, he pouted, his brother had the time and a car that was much newer than his own crumbling jalopy.

Exiting the 7-Eleven, Seymour suddenly grew dizzy again and this time could not keep himself from toppling to the pavement. He was certain someone had plunged an axe into his skull. Then he felt nothing. There were voices from somewhere in the darkness that enveloped him, but he could not understand what they were saying. Nor could he respond.

*   *   *

Gil sat beside his brother's bed in the hospital's ICU. According to the attending doctor, Seymour had suffered a stroke caused by a blood clot. He had been tended to by the EMTs outside the convenience store. While this sounded very dire to Gil, the physician indicated that the clot had been taken care of and that there was every reason to believe his brother would soon be fine. At the moment he was in a medically induced coma to calm the trauma caused by the clot and surgery.

"How long will he be unconscious?" asked, Gil, still jarred by what had befallen his younger sibling.

"Not totally sure, maybe a couple of days . . . four or five at the most. His vitals are good. He was very lucky. Should be okay. Don't expect any paralysis."

"Thank God," said Gil, sighing.

In his foggy mind, Seymour heard muffled voices. He could not determine if his eyes were open or shut, since he was unable to move his lids or touch them. He was immobilized, yet what was happening aroused more curiosity than any sense of foreboding. Then the seemingly distant sounds faded as he floated in a starless sky—a gently rocking motion soothing him. In the encompassing blackness appeared a speck of light that slowly gained substance and morphed into countless iridescent lines and circles that pulsated and spun around him.

"Seymour," beckoned a softly compelling voice.

The geometric shapes fell away, leaving in their wake a field awash in bright flowers.

"Who . . .?" asked Seymour, finding that his voice had returned. "What is it . . .?"

"Look," replied the disembodied voice. "Over here, beyond the willows. You're home."

Seymour moved his eyes across the colorful landscape and saw a picturesque two-story cottage. A figure beckoned him from its trellised doorway.

It's a woman, thought Seymour, and his heart filled with joy. He knew he loved her.

Two small children emerged from the house and waved excitedly at him.

"Daddy," they called, and Seymour looked around to see if they were addressing someone else.

He then realized they were *his* children and this brought tears to his eyes. Ardent embraces awaited Seymour when he reached them.

"You've been gone so long, dear. We're so happy you're back. Dinner is on the table," said the woman acting for all the world like his spouse.

Her beauty caused him to become faint for a moment. She was the very woman he had always fantasized marrying. Every aspect of her being was perfect to him. Her warm smile ignited his affection and passion.

"Sweetheart," he whispered in her ear. "I've missed you."

That evening, after the children were lovingly tucked away, Seymour and his magnificent consort retired to the bedroom. As he lay on the bed, the woman of his dreams removed her clothes and stood naked before him. The vision of her perfect body was too much for Seymour and he could not contain his sobs of gratitude for what had been given him.

* * *

"Nurse . . . nurse, he's making a noise. I think he's crying," shouted Gil, as he stared down at his brother.

"He's coming out of the coma," reported the nurse, arriving at the scene.

"Why's he crying? Is he in pain?" inquired Gil.

"Coma patients return to consciousness in all kinds of ways. Some laugh hysterically, others scream and wave their arms frantically. Some even sing and quote Shakespeare. Mostly they just open their eyes though. Criers like him are fairly rare," observed the nurse, checking Seymour's vitals on the monitors.

Within hours, Seymour was sitting up and showing signs of a full recovery, according to his attending physician.

"So he'll be able to come home soon?" inquired Gil.

"I'd say in a day or two if all goes the way I expect it will," answered the doctor, beaming at his patient.

"I don't want to come home," argued Seymour.

"What do you mean?" inquired his brother, mystified.

"I liked it there . . . ."

"There . . .where?" asked the doctor and Gil in unison.

"With my wi . . ." responded Seymour, catching himself mid-sentence. "I mean I'd like to go somewhere else."

"You'll be happy to be home," offered Gil.

"It's not my home. My home is with . . . .. Oh, never mind," muttered Seymour, frustrated.

"Look, it's normal for someone who's been through what you have to feel a bit disjointed and out of sorts, but you're in pretty good physical health and this medical event will quickly recede in your mind," assured the doctor, checking his watch. "I'll be by in the morning to check your progress. We'll spring you from this joint soon."

* * *

And so it was. Three days later, Seymour was back home where he was told to remain for a couple of weeks before returning to work. During this period, his brother reverted to form, providing minimal assistance, and only a handful of meals.

When his convalescence was over, Seymour actually looked forward to returning to work, but his enthusiasm was short-lived as the numbing routine of his job once again depressed his spirits. His thoughts kept returning to the adoring family he'd found while unconscious, and his longing for them grew in intensity. If he'd had the choice to return to that perfect otherworld, he would do so without a second thought. Everything he ever wanted was there. *Was it only a dream?* Seymour wondered, as he sat at the picnic table with his usual bag lunch before him.

"You okay, buddy?" asked Mark Hiller, standing across from Seymour. "Mind if I join you? I've decided to drop a few pounds, so I'm eating rabbit food."

"The Gout Brigade will miss you," quipped Seymour, reaching into his brown satchel that contained his noonday meal.

"Baloney?" asked Mark, nodding at Seymour's sandwich.

"Tuna," answered Seymour, whose eyes suddenly rolled back into his head.

"Jesus, Seymour, what's the matter?" asked Mark, quickly moving to catch Seymour as he began to fall backward.

* * *

"He's had what's called a focal cerebral ischemia stemming from a lack of oxygen to his brain during his last stroke," responded the doctor to Gil's inquiry.

"Why? What does that mean? Is he going to come out of it?"

"These things are not uncommon, but their outcome is a bit hard to predict. Many patients soon regain consciousness. However, damage to some neurons will be irreversible. Some physical therapy is usually required to regain motor skills when they regain consciousness. On the other hand, the results could be different, Mr. Bauls. We'll just have to see what happens. He could be under for months."

This time, Seymour could understand the words he heard while inside the void he occupied. The doctor's statement filled him with anticipation. *I'll be reunited with my wife and children*, he thought. He waited anxiously to see the spec of light that had presaged his extraordinary experience in his first coma, but it failed to appear.

Weeks passed as Seymour's desperation to reclaim his dream got the better of him. *It was just a sad man's pathetic fantasy*, he concluded.

In the hospital room where he lay unresponsively for weeks, his brother was informed that his sibling was failing.

"Doesn't seem like he's got much fight left in him. His system is shutting down, and I don't think he's got much longer," reported Seymour's doctor.

"But I thought you said he'd come out of it and be okay," protested Gil.

"That's usually the case, but your brother hasn't shown any signs of recovery, especially lately. At first, he seemed to be improving...slightly, but in the last few weeks there's been no gains, and now he's deteriorating quickly. I'm sorry, Mr. Bauls. We've done what we can. In these cases, recovery is often more up to the patient than we medicos."

When the doctor departed, Gil whispered emotionally charged words of encouragement into Seymour's ear, but he heard nothing. A week later, Seymour's brain scan flat lined and no attempt was made to resuscitate him per his living will.

"My condolences, Mr. Bauls."

"No problem, doc. He's probably in a better place," replied Gil, gloomily.

* * *

At the instant Seymour's heart stopped, he found himself standing before the cottage of his beloved family.

"*Thank you . . . thank you,*" he muttered, looking upward as he swung the door open.

As he stepped inside, he saw someone in the dim interior and excitedly moved forward.

"Sweetheart, I'm back, and I'll never leave," he called out, joyously.

"My love?" answered a quavering voice, and from the shadows emerged an elderly woman who faintly resembled his once beautiful wife. "You've been gone for so long, but now we'll be together forever."

Seymour stood silently for several moments and then smiled tenderly at the stooped figure before him with whom he would spend eternity.

"Okay," he shrugged. "*Okay* . . .."

Alme

The desert has its secrets, and some are wonderful.
—Curtis Frederick

Word reached Acyl Kabadi that his father was gravely ill. At once he prepared to make the journey to Koro Toro, sixty-seven kilometers from his tiny village in the deep Sahara. His twelve-year-old son, Ngia, would accompany him on the trek that would take them four days on foot. They had no other means of transportation, since their camel had recently been stricken with lungworm. Given that their neighbors were about to depart for the bazaar in Oum-Chalouba, there was not one to be borrowed, either.

Before the sun rose above the flat horizon, they set out, leaving Ngia's mother, Dyese, and sister, Achta, to join the other villagers on their thrice annual sojourn to the marketplace. There they would peddle their handmade jewelry and leather goods and purchase essential supplies for the coming months.

By noon the next day, Acyl and Ngia had traveled far into the Djourab basin. It was there that the sky lost its color, stained by swirling sand. As they made their way across a stretch of dunes, the wind intensified and soon their visibility was lost.

"We will stop and shield ourselves, my son. Come, let us gather in until the storm is over," shouted Acyl, who fought to wrap his body in a white kaftan he planned to wear when greeting his father. "Ngia!" he called again, but there was no answer, as his son was beyond the reach of his voice.

The strong blasts of sand stung Ngia's face and drew tears to his eyes as he called out for his father. The only thing either could hear was the din of the ferocious *haboob*. Ngia was no stranger to the Sahara storms, but he had never experienced one as powerful as the one that now separated him from his father.

Ngia burrowed into the dune and formed into a ball to keep from being battered. There in the darkness he waited out the storm, hoping it would soon end and he could find his father. Despite shielding himself, Ngia found that the insidious sand had made its way deep inside his mouth. He attempted to spit but he had no saliva, and when he swallowed it felt as if stones were lodged in his throat. His breathing became so difficult that for a time he thought he would suffocate.

Just as things seemed hopeless, the sand and wind settled, and Ngia dug himself from the dune and scoured the landscape for signs of his father. Everything had been transformed by the storm. The dunes had been reconfigured, making his surroundings appear unfamiliar. Ngia was disoriented and had no sense of the direction in which he and his father had traveled before the dusty onslaught.

"Baba!" called Ngia, until his parched throat gave out.

There was no sign of his father as he carefully searched for him from atop the highest dune he could mount. His thirst was growing, but he had not carried water. At least his father would have something to drink, and that thought comforted Ngia as he removed sand from his eyes, ears, and nostrils.

The sky remained the color of the desert. As long as the sun was concealed, Ngia could not get his bearings to return home or continue to the place of his ailing grandfather. By the time the sky had cleared and the sun was visible, Ngia had decided to press on with his travel to Koro Toro. It would be what his father would do, and he believed his parent would wish him to do likewise. He fervently hoped they would meet along the way.

* * *

It was nightfall when Ngia reached the edge of the dunes and was able to move without his feet sinking into the sand with every step. Although the solid ground would allow him to move more swiftly, he was exhausted from hours of dragging his legs through the mounds of sand. He located a large rock and nestled against it, unaware it was home to a family of fox. As quickly as he went to sleep, he was awakened by something licking his feet. He let out a scream and a baby fennec scooted away. Ngia decided to find another place to sleep quickly locating what he thought a more suitable resting area next to a large Welwitchsia plant. Its leaves felt cool against Ngia's skin, and he promptly returned to his dreams.

Before the sun rose, Ngia was awakened by ant bites on his neck and legs. He leapt to his feet and frantically brushed the insects from his body.

"Baba!" he called loudly, as he moved away from his infested bed.

There remained no response to his desperate summons. As the eastern sky brightened, Ngia began to move in the direction of what he hoped would take him to his grandfather's home. He had never felt such thirst, and he experienced tremendous weakness as he walked across what would soon be a blistering surface.

"Baba, baba," he muttered, stumbling more than striding.

It was not long before what little energy he had was gone, and he collapsed to the desiccated soil. When he struck the ground, his hand touched something strange, and he pulled it away anxiously. After a moment, he dared to make contact with the object again. It reminded Ngia of a dried goat stomach that his mother made into carrying pouches, but it felt coarser. As Ngia lifted his head for a look, he became dizzy and lost consciousness. When he came to, cool water was washing over his body.

"Baba, baba!" he bellowed, expectantly, but when his eyes cleared, he beheld an elephant.

At first, he was frightened, but then he recalled a favorite story told by a village elder in which a man had touched the skin of a deceased elephant only to have it come to life and grant him a wish. The man had asked for the ability to sire children, something he had not been able to do, and soon he and his wife were blessed by a dozen offspring.

"Tembo, please find my father," pleaded Ngia, and the pachyderm lifted him to his back with his trunk and carried him away.

From his elevated perch, he soon spotted his father and directed the elephant to trumpet a signal to gain his attention. The loud sound startled Acyl, who then returned his son's excited wave.

"Where did you get this wondrous animal, Ngia?" asked his father, looking up at his son.

"It is like the tale, baba. I touched the skin and it appeared," explained Ngia. "Climb up with me and we can travel to see dear, sick oupa."

The elephant extended its trunk to Acyl and lifted him to his son. When it was dusk, they alighted and spent the night amid a cluster of date palms. In the morning, they discovered that the elephant was gone. A piece of its skin lay on the ground where it had stood the night before. This alarmed both Acyl and Ngia, for they felt it was a sign that their fate would hold further sorrows.

"Baba, look!" shouted Ngia, pointing toward the south.

"It's Koro Toro," declared his father, relieved.

Ngia rolled up the piece of elephant skin and tucked it beneath his darija. He and his father then set off for the town, which they calculated was less than six kilometers away.

"Will grandfather die?" asked Ngia.

"He is very ill, and the healer is no longer able to make him well, my son."

* * *

When Acyl and Ngia arrived at the elder Kabadi's mud brick dwelling, they were shocked and delighted to find him sitting on its doorstep looking robust.

"Oupa, we fear you were dying," said Ngia, befuddled.

"No, no," laughed his grandfather. "I found magic to heal me. Look," he said, removing an object from his cloak and setting it on a small wooden crate.

"It is my elephant skin!" exclaimed Ngia, searching his clothing for it. "It is gone, baba! It is not where I kept it!"

As he spoke, it began to rain hard—something very much out of season. The Kadabises rejoiced for the wonderful relief it provided them. When the refreshing cloudburst ended, they noticed that the elephant skin had vanished.

Grandfather, father, and son stared in amazement at the crate where it had been only moments before.

"*Magic* tembo," declared Ngia, with a broad grin, and the jubilant Kadabises sang songs of praise and thanks as another wave of cooling droplets descended from the cloudless sky.

Handy

Agatha was born

with an umbrella handle in her nose.

She was scorned and ridiculed

until it rained.

How Chris Morgan Became a Street Person

Now slides the silent meteor on . . .
—Lord Tennyson

"It's just a matter of time before the human race is obliterated," proclaimed Chris Morgan, to his small group of friends ensconced on his living room couch. "We don't stand a chance with the billions of space rocks flying around us. My God, they say a piece of debris the size of a football field could annihilate us, and we're sitting ducks. It's going to happen, and experts say we're overdue for a hit."

"And what exactly are we supposed to do with that charming bit of information, Chris?" asked David Belgrade, one of Chris's oldest friends.

"Eat, drink, and be merry, I guess," responded the gathering's host.

"You sure know how to perk up a party," added Matt O'Connor, dipping a chip into what remained of the hummus.

"Well, I got your attention, didn't I?"

"You sure did, but I think I'd rather you take another approach to livening up things the next time," balked O'Connor, checking his watch. "Whoa, it's after midnight. I'm up early tomorrow, so I'm out of here."

Chris's three other guests rose from the couch with O'Connor and made their farewells, too. After their departure, Chris tidied up and went to bed, but sleep evaded him. *We are sitting ducks*, he thought, as images of a fiery comet plunging toward Earth kept him hot-wired.

Over the coming weeks, Chris's preoccupation with the doomsday scenario grew to an obsession. It was not a new concern of his, but lately it had occupied more and more of his thoughts. He now spent all of his available time on the various websites that proclaimed a rogue comet would soon strike Earth, wiping out all of its life forms. There was nothing else he cared to talk about, and he soon taxed the patience of his friends and relatives.

"I think you should get some help," advised David Belgrade. "You got a problem here, buddy."

"Why, because I realize something the rest of you seem oblivious to?"

"Fine, but it's not healthy to eat, drink, and sleep it. Besides, you're really freaking people out. Not about the big collision, but in the way you get all frothed up and rave on. You're like that minister who keeps predicting Armageddon, and he hasn't been too accurate, has he?"

"Okay, I won't alert people to what's going to happen. You know, it's not a bad thing I'm doing . . . letting people know that the endgame is approaching. Lets folks get their lives in order. Tell their kids they love them and stuff," said Chris, defensively.

"Look, I know you think you're doing the right thing and all, but you're sounding wacky, and it's not doing you any good, especially here at work."

"You're like the rest. You just don't realize what's about to happen. If not today or tomorrow, but soon . . . *soon*," persisted Chris.

"I'm telling you that it's getting you in trouble. The boss is not happy," warned David.

"Fine. Got it. I'll stop warning people about the comet here at work, okay? I mean if that makes you feel better."

"Just looking out for you, Chris. You might put the subject on hiatus everywhere for a while, too."

Try as he might, however, Chris could not get the approaching comet out of his head, nor could he stop alerting people about its approach. And, as David predicted, less than a week after their conversation, he was fired. Citing his behavior as disruptive to the work place, his superior, Karen Bolling, instructed him to clear out his desk immediately.

"You'll get a month's severance pay and six months of health coverage. I'd advise you to take advantage of the latter and seek some counseling, Chris. You have an issue that needs to be addressed. I'm sorry it had to come to this."

"Well, I'm sorry you think that what I've been saying around here is *disruptive*, but you'll know what real disruption is soon enough," countered Chris, as a security guard appeared at the door.

"John will accompany you as you gather up your things and leave the building," announced Bolling, signaling that the conversation was over.

Chris was more amused than upset. *The end of the human race is coming and no one wants to hear about it. Well, screw them all,* he thought as he exited the software manufacturing company where he had spent the last decade as a programmer. *It's all going to be over soon, so who needs a job?* he muttered to his uniformed escort.

* * *

Within a few weeks, the phone had all but stopped ringing and his friends were not answering his emails as he holed up in his apartment. No invitations to meet up with people were forthcoming either. His only contact with outsiders was through the handful of blogs devoted to discussing the onrushing space object. These blogs claimed that the government was keeping secret information about the giant meteor—what it called The Demolisher—for fear it would induce widespread panic.

"What the hell does it matter what it causes?" grumbled Chris. "It's all going to be over when it hits anyway."

Chris was startled when his cellphone finally rang. He could see by caller ID that it was David.

About time, he mumbled, answering the phone.

"Hey, Chris. You okay? Thought I'd drop in for a little visit."

"Well, I'm still breathing," quipped Chris, detecting the worry in his friend's voice. "Sure, come on by. I haven't had too many visitors lately."

An hour later, David arrived carrying a six-pack of Molson, a bag of Doritos, and a jar of salsa.

"Figure you need some nourishment."

"Yeah, nothing like some good healthy snacks," quipped Chris, adding, "But I don't think we have to worry about extending our longevity."

"You still on that kick, I see," replied David, not concealing his disappointment and concern.

"Yeah, and it's going to be a hell of a kick, too. Right across the galaxy through the uprights of eternity."

"That's a pretty heavy analogy. See you haven't lost your flare for rhetoric."

"All the information about it is out there on the Internet if people would just take the time to read it," replied Chris, with exasperation.

"What crazy sites have you been Googling? You ever try NASA? They're the authority on stuff like this. Look, I made a copy from their site on the subject of Earth's chances of being hit by a comet."

David unfolded a piece of paper and proceeded to read from it: "We know nothing currently about a comet colliding with Earth, and the chances are virtually nil of anything striking the planet of comparable size that ended the existence of the dinosaurs."

Chris shrugged his shoulders dismissively.

"They're being censored by the national security agencies of the government. Believe me, they know the truth."

"Oh, come on, Chris. For *chrissakes*, you can't believe this," sighed David.

It didn't take him long to feel the urge to leave his friend's apartment. It was the same old conversation, and he had heard enough. David could not help but notice that most of the kitchen table and counters were covered with print-outs from the Internet sites where Chris had been spending so much time.

"You'd be better off checking out some job sites, like CareerBuilders.com or Monster.com. You said you had no savings, so your funds must be getting down there," advised David.

"I plan to," replied Chris, slightly irritated by his friend's suggestion.

After an awkward silence, David made an excuse to leave, and both men shook hands goodbye.

* * *

Chris ignored his friend's proposal that he look for work, considering that doing so was foolish in the extreme, with the planet's life clock rapidly running down. The reality of his bleak financial situation was driven home when he was soon informed that he had to vacate his apartment because of two months unpaid back rent.

He rejected the notion of moving in with his parents or any of his relatives on the grounds that they had proven the most skeptical of his conviction that a deadly comet would soon inflict its malice on the planet. After mulling the situation over, he contacted David and asked if he could crash at his apartment until he found a job. Of course, he had no intention of seeking employment, given his belief in the futility of such an exercise in the face of imminent doom.

Reluctantly, David agreed that Chris could stay with him temporarily only if he promised not to mention anything about his killer comet theory. For the first few days of their shared habitation, things seemed to be going along pretty well, but then Chris returned to his obsessive ranting about the impending impact with The Demolisher.

"You're out of here, man," shouted David. "I can't take it. Go to your parents' house. They'll take you in. You know that. I just can't deal with you. I told you to get some help. Shit, everybody told you that, but you won't, so what can we do, huh?"

David gathered up the few belongings Chris had brought with him to his apartment and attempted to give him a twenty-dollar bill for cab fare to his parents.

"Keep your money. I'm fine. And I'm not throwing in with my mom and dad either. They don't believe a thing I say, either. Like the time when I was a kid and they wouldn't . . . .."

"Wouldn't what?"

"It doesn't matter. Never mind. They're nuts," pouted Chris, after a pause.

David was tempted to say he wasn't surprised that the Morgans were nuts given the child they had sired, but he kept silent as Chris left his apartment.

* * *

Without enough money to pay for a hotel room, Chris spent the night in the Port Authority bus station. Around three in the morning, transit police roused sleeping vagrants and turned them out into the cold. Chris was among them. The frigid wind whipped through the canyons of the city's skyscrapers and he sought out an entrance where he could reduce his exposure to the elements.

There he awaited the arrival of dawn without a plan to address his situation. *The Demolisher will take care of everything,* he thought, as the icy air drew tears from his eyes.

While Chris anticipated the world's demise, he spent his days wandering Manhattan, dodging in and out of stores and office buildings to get warm. The hurried and resolute activity of the human race struck him as senseless, in view of what he knew lay just around the corner. He had no desire to rejoin the ebb and flow of the doomed planet's inhabitants and was content to spend his remaining time observing the folly of human endeavor.

People are blind. They just don't want to face reality, he thought, as he watched the endless throngs of men and women dashing about in every direction. Although Chris no longer had access to the Internet to update himself on the imminent strike from space, he was certain it was merely a heartbeat away.

During the weeks he spent roaming the city he had settled on a place to spend the chilly nights. In the bushes near the memorial in Central Park called Strawberry Fields, Chris covered himself with layers of old newspapers and peeked out from his makeshift bed to the star-speckled sky. *Nothing is forever, right, John?* he mumbled as his eyes were drawn to a stunning flaming object hurtling toward Earth. *Nothing,* he repeated, smiling knowingly.

Several days later, a man walking his dog discovered Chris's half-frozen body.

Wanda Love Bobby

*Youths green and happy in first love,
so thankful for illusion.*
—Arthur Hugh Clough

Nothing made Wanda Howell happier than when the local oldies station played songs by her favorite singer of all time, Bobby Rydell. It was not only his voice that lifted her spirits, but she considered him the best-looking man in the world. In fact, she had been totally smitten by Rydell since first seeing him on *American Bandstand* in the late 1950s. Despite the passing decades, the teen idol never aged in Wanda's mind, which had been oxygen deprived at birth, seriously impairing her cognitive abilities. With an IQ in the 60s, Wanda's range of interests was limited, but her enthusiasm for the few things she enjoyed was boundless. For twenty-seven years, she had resided in a group home on the outskirts of Kearney, Nebraska, only five miles from where her parents had lived until their deaths. Her winsome disposition endeared her to the staff of the facility, which did everything it could to make her life comfortable and fulfilling. This was not a challenge since having her favorite ice cream (butter pecan) on hand and reserving a front row seat in the television room for her to watch *General Hospital* were all she appeared to need—in addition to her beloved Bobby Rydell cassettes. Wanda had every recording ever made by Rydell, but she could not get enough of two particular songs—"The Cha-Cha-Cha" and "Volare."

At most hours, she could be seen dancing to the tunes in her small room just off the lobby. Staff members often joined her as she swirled around her bed and on occasion they would spill into the hall to the mild bemusement of the home's director, Kyle Livingston, who feared they might collide with other residents. Secretly, however, he thought the romping was harmless and probably a morale booster for everyone—staff and residents alike. Indeed, he had come to feel great affection for Wanda over the years that he managed the home.

At first, he found her demeanor and limited repartee irritating, but in time he came to regard her as a model resident, since she caused no problem and actually lifted the mood and atmosphere of the facility. Her contagious effervescence made her something of a beloved mascot—an ambassador of goodwill—at Kearney House. Over the years, Wanda's room had become a virtual shrine to her idol. Every inch of wall space was covered with posters and photos of the young Rydell, and every time someone passed her room, she would invariably invite them in to admire her precious collection.

"See, Bobby!" she would shout to passersby, and most would simply wave as they passed, having heard her invitation countless times.

Wanda's friendly summons was always followed by the words "Wanda love Bobby" and the lyrics to one of Rydell's hits. Although she could barely connect two cogent sentences during a conversation, she performed the songs flawlessly and always with great zeal. At Christmas time, she did get on some people's nerves by repeatedly singing Rydell's version of "Jingle Bell Rock."

"Can't you sing 'Silent Night' or 'Frosty the Snowman,' sweetie?" the receptionist, Bernice Webster, would plead, doing her best to turn a deaf ear to Wanda's perseveration, because she, like everyone else in the facility, cared for her and did not want to hurt her feelings.

"Wanda love Bobby," she would respond, continuing her ceaseless rendition of the holiday staple. For several days following her sixty-fourth birthday, Wanda complained of extreme abdominal pain. Eventually, she was taken to the hospital where an ex-ray revealed an object lodged in her lower intestine, which was quickly removed. To everyone's surprise it was a partially masticated photo of Bobby Rydell. When Kearney House staff inspected Wanda's bedroom walls, they noticed several spaces where photos of her idol had previously hung. After a couple of days, Wanda was returned home, but she was not her usual sunny self, spending most her time in bed and eating little. Staff believed her gloomy mood was the result of their removing all edible pictures from her room. Each time she was visited by concerned staff, she would mournfully moan "Wanda love Bobby."

When some facility personnel suggested that the pictures be returned, Kyle Livingston was disinclined to comply, fearing Wanda would again attempt to devour them. Despite this, Wanda's loyal caregivers continued to pressure Livingston to do what they felt would restore her to her previous disposition.

* * *

The Tuesday after Wanda's return from the hospital, Bernice noticed that Bobby Rydell was actually scheduled to perform live at the Kearney County Fair two days hence. She immediately sprang into action to get the singer to visit Wanda, figuring that it may overcome her deepening funk. To her great satisfaction, the crooner agreed to show up at Kearney House at a designated time, and true to his word, he did so punctually.

"This will mean so much to Wanda," said Bernice to the graying and paunchy balladeer, whose winning smile had changed little since his heyday.

"Always happy to help a fan. Show me the way," said Rydell, who was then escorted to Wanda's room by both the receptionist and Kyle.

"We'll stay out here, so the focus is just on you," said Bernice.

"Well, maybe we should accompany Mr. Rydell," protested Kyle, prompting Bernice to grab his arm.

"We'll be right here in the hall, Mr. Rydell, if you need anything," said Bernice firmly.

"Okay," replied Kyle, reluctantly allowing Rydell to access the room on his own. A moment after the singer entered it, a deafening scream occurred.

"Old man! Get out . . . help! Old man!" shrieked Wanda, as Rydell ran from her room.

"As soon as she saw me, she went bonkers," reported Rydell, the color drained from his lined face.

Kyle and Bernice calmed Wanda while the singer stood dejected in the hall. They then thanked him for his effort and escorted him to an awaiting taxi.

"She really loves you, Mr. Rydell, said Bernice apologetically.

"Yeah, I could tell. My fans always react like that when they see me," he responded, with a reassuring wink. For the rest of the day, Wanda remained in an agitated state finally falling asleep to the soothing chords of "Childhood Sweetheart."

While Wanda slept, Kyle placed two photos of Rydell inside plexi-glass picture frames and instructed the facility's custodian to secure them to the wall of her room. When Bernice and Kyle arrived at work the next morning, they were greeted by the strains of "The Cha-Cha-Cha."

"How are you, Wanda?" asked Kyle, poking his head into her room on his way to his office.

"See Bobby," she replied, standing before the photos of her young dream lover. Wanda love Bobby . . . Wanda *love* Bobby."

The Sweetening

One should eat to live, and not live to eat.
—Moliere

As residents of a troubled planet in the HCM 6A galaxy, the Torgosians had studied data on Earthlings for eons. They knew that one day they might have to make contact with the inhabitants of the blue planet to insure the continuation of life on Torgos. They finally implemented their eleventh hour plan in hopes that all would go well.

Unlike all predecessors—who had invariably traumatized humans during alien expeditions to Earth—the Torgosians would treat the Earthlings with kindness and understanding. There would be no abductions or anal probes but rather actions designed to attract the primitive species and thus insure their cooperation and usefulness. Evidence gathered by explorers from other worlds had proved that humanoids would serve no purpose if poisoned by fear and apprehension. Indeed, the Torgosians' mission would fail, resulting in catastrophe.

"Earthlings are *the* answer, my fellow Torgosians, so we must proceed according to the knowledge we have gathered for so long. We must make them like us. Only then shall we have what they alone can provide for our preservation. We cannot disturb their delicate molecular structures with intimidation. It will spoil everything," declared Supreme Master Coheb Koofla, just prior to the launch of the mission to the Milky Way Galaxy, billions of miles from Torgos.

Failure to achieve their objective would mean the end of their species, so it was with the utmost resolve and urgency that twenty massive vessels—each with a crew of one thousand—departed their world in pursuit of the final solution.

* * *

In 2,400 wextars (two months in human time), the Torgosians reached Earth, landing in different and far-flung reaches of the planet. From there, they set out to befriend the indigenous population in order to convince as many humans as possible to return with them to Torgos.

To meet this challenge, the Torgosians assumed the form of Earthlings and engaged in a vast array of earthly social activities in associations and groups of every conceivable type. Their target demographic was young men and women as well as pubescent children. The Torgosians had earlier determined that Earth's elders would not sufficiently meet their needs. Freshness was a vital criterion.

As part of the preparation for their expedition, ships' crews had been schooled in what subjects would most engage humans. The list of discussion topics included, among others, television, food, sports events, clothing, guns, cars, vacations, movies, sex, beer, candy, money, Botox, cellphones, tobacco, pop music, war, and amusement parks. All of these talking points were to be used to gain the Earthlings' trust and camaraderie.

"These are favorite conversation topics for the creatures of this incipient orb. They are . . ." Supreme Master Koofla hesitated as he perused a scroll held by four of his twelve limbs, "ice breakers. Yes . . . they are *icebreakers*."

The vast assembly squealed loudly at the exotic term while its leader nodded its heads in satisfaction.

"You are to show . . ." again the Torgosian chief searched for the right word, "*love* to these lower life forms, so they may conform to your will. They have a maxim 'You attract more bees with honey than with vinegar.' So *you* must be the honey, and then they will swarm to you. We need them. They are our salvation," continued Koofla, to louder squeals.

Thus, it was with a wave of the leader's glowing scepter, that twenty thousand Torgosians had left their imperiled planet for the fruits of another.

* * *

In a matter of days, the Torgosians had made great strides in befriending Earthlings. By focusing on what humans wanted to hear, the disguised visitors quickly attained remarkable popularity. Their end game involved revealing their extraterrestrial identity, but only after obtaining the complete confidence of their intended benefactors. Humans would not be forced to leave their planet, because this was shown to sour them and make them bitter. Instead they would provide Earthlings with ample reasons to emigrate. Among their many promises were holographic television implants, weight reducing junk food, vitamin enhanced cigarettes, non-invasive colonoscopies, endless cellphone minutes, unlimited vacations, champion sports teams, chemical stimulants, and multiple orgasms. To the profound satisfaction of the Torgosians, most of the befriended Earthlings were thrilled to accept the proposition.

More than a million humans were beamed onto the awaiting Torgosian spaceships. Once aboard they found the accommodations exceeded their wildest expectations. Each voyager was escorted to a luxurious leather recliner, replete with cup holders containing super-sized beverages and trays laden with heaps of mouth-watering salty snacks. Cheers of joy echoed through the passenger compartments of the space-born carriers. During the journey, humans were provided with anything they desired. Nothing was denied them, and they came to venerate their hosts.

"We are so lucky to be given this opportunity," was the common exchange between humans—all of whom gained considerable weight on the voyage.

Some of the men and women travelers believed they were part of the Rapture—the Chosen ones—as prophesied by a sect of the Christian faith. This conviction only heightened the euphoria of these Torgos-bound Earthlings.

The Torgosians could not have been more pleased as well. They would soon deliver their precious cargo to their awaiting brethren. As the ships made their final approach to their home base, the Earthlings grew excited to begin their new lives, thankful that they were the chosen ones. Some believed that they were being taken to heaven, although they were understandably curious how this was possible, since they were still alive.

"It is the triumphant day of arrival," declared the captain of each ship, "and it is with great gratitude that you have agreed to bless us with your presence. Considering your sacrifice, this is especially momentous."

With those words, the crafts' spiraled levels filled with waiting excited passengers began to rotate. At the same time, the humans began to experience intense heat, but to their relief, the air was filled with a cool, mellifluent mist.

"It is sweet like honey," observed many voyagers.

"Yes," remarked others, "like . . . *barbecue sauce?!*"

Brief screams began to fill the depleting oxygen as flesh reddened, blistered, bubbled, and cracked, splattering body juices in all directions. Each of the human cargo holds in the Torgosians ships had been transformed into rotisserie cookers.

Ecstatic squeals greeted the returning vessels as they landed with the life-sustaining nourishment.

As the Torgosians feasted, more ships were launched toward Earth.

Infantasy

Hence, dear delusion, sweet enchantment, hence!
—James Smith

Paul Morgan squeezed his wailing infant grandson tighter and tighter as he stood trembling with rage in the kitchen doorway. He was overwhelmed with the urge to heave the baby toward the floor. *Shut up!* bellowed his inner voice. He was a split second away from committing the heinous crime when reason took over, sparing the child and grandfather a tragic fate.

The realization of what he had almost done horrified him and made him swoon. *Oh my God*, he shrieked to himself. *Oh my God!*

"Here, take him . . . take him!" blurted Paul to his wife, who had not witnessed her husband's near meltdown.

"Okay, okay. What's the matter? You all right?"

"Just feeling a little nauseous," replied Paul, practically shoving the child into his wife's arms and dashing to the bathroom.

"Come to nana, my little sweetheart. Don't cry," cooed Julie Morgan, gently rocking her grandson, Danny Jason Howell, in her arms.

Paul stared at himself in the medicine cabinet mirror trying to come to grips with what had just happened, or what had nearly happened. "I almost killed him," he muttered, shaking his head in total revulsion. "I almost killed him."

Then his stomach erupted, spilling its contents into the sink.

"Honey, is everything all right?" called his wife, hearing his abject moans.

After a long pause, Paul emerged from the bathroom wiping his mouth with tissue paper.

"Think I might have a touch of the stomach flu," he offered to divert his wife's curiosity over his peculiar behavior.

"Oh, dear. Well, you better stay away from the baby. We don't want him to get sick."

Paul looked at the now sleeping newborn in his wife's arms and fought back tears.

"Papa loves his little Danny boy," Paul swallowed hard. "He would never let anything hurt him . . . *never.*"

* * *

In the days that followed, Paul obsessed over his near act of infanticide. He knew he had been terribly stressed out by the substantial loss of his retirement savings on a stupid investment. The setback had greatly altered his mood, and rightfully so, but the idea that his anger and frustration over it had brought him so close to committing the unthinkable haunted him. He vowed never to allow himself to reach that point again but could not exorcise the image of what almost occurred. His grandson's body smashing against the kitchen floor played over and over in his mind and increased his self-loathing. Each time the ghastly phantasm asserted itself, Paul would deride his existence. *I am a demon . . . an evil person. Oh, God, I almost killed the baby. I don't deserve to live . . ..*

Paul realized that he could not admit to anyone how close he had come to slaughtering his grandson, but he felt a profound need to make amends for his fleeting urge. Thus he resolved to show Danny every possible kindness as the boy grew into adulthood. There would be nothing he would not do to make his life better. He believed this was the only way to make up for almost destroying him. Over the next few months, Paul doted endlessly on the infant, plying him with lavish affection and buying him every new toy he could lay his hands on.

"Daddy, we don't have any more space in his room for everything you've given him," remarked his daughter, Megan, as Paul hauled in yet another oversized stuffed animal.

"My little Danny boy can't have too many gifts from his old grandpa," replied Paul.

"It's nice of you, but pretty soon we won't have a path to his crib if you keep buying him things."

"Maybe he'd like a pony," Paul half-joked to his daughter.

"I think he needs to be able to sit up on his own first," answered Danny's mother, rolling her eyes in feigned frustration. "Or maybe you should just get him a car. Why wait until he's sixteen?"

"Hmmm . . . good idea," retorted Paul.

When Danny reached his first birthday, his grandfather hired a menagerie of circus animals and a magician and insisted his daughter invite as many children as she could to his party. Each subsequent birthday was an even more extravagant event than the last. Paul approached his grandson's birthdays with the utmost solemnity because each represented another year the child had survived his near annihilation at the hands of his grandfather.

"Papa loves his birthday boy," he would whisper into Danny's ear throughout the annual events.

"What do you keep saying to him, Daddy?" asked Megan.

"That his papa loves him."

"Jeez, I think he knows that, daddy."

"Well, I just want to make sure, honey. You can never tell a child you love him too much," said Paul, and as he looked at his grandson adoringly the nightmare image of what might have been flickered across his mind's eye yet again, chasing the glee from his heart.

* * *

As Danny grew older, Paul was always at his side taking great interest in the child's welfare and development. He attended every sporting event and music recital in which his grandson participated, enthusiastically cheering him on. It was Paul's declared mission to make the boy's life—one he had nearly taken—as ideal as possible. The guilt he felt over what he had nearly done to his grandson remained deeply rooted in his being, all too often dominating his thoughts. His absolute devotion to Danny aroused criticism, if not envy, in his wife, who he had come to neglect because of his total commitment to his grandson.

"I don't see why I can't come with you and Danny," pouted Julie, when Paul announced plans to take his grandson on a week-long hiking trip.

"It's his eighth birthday, and you know I promised to take him down part of the Appalachian Trail when he was old enough. Besides, it's a guy thing. No women allowed," replied Paul, attempting to mitigate his wife's dour mood.

"You spoil him so much. Everything is for Danny. I love him, too, but there *is* a limit, My God, you act as if he's the only person on earth. You're so driven when it comes to him."

"I just want him to have a great childhood," defended Paul.

"Well, that's not your sole responsibility. We all want him to be happy, and we do what we can to make that happen, but you're just too excessive," Julie responded.

"Look, we'll take him to Disney World together for his next birthday, okay? This hiking trip is something I promised him, so I can't change things now. He's really looking forward to it."

"Well, it's not like you don't do anything with him. Good lord, you've spent every available minute with him since he was born. You act like you're trying to be the only person in his life, the center of his universe. Super Grandpa."

"They grow up fast and then it's like they never were a child. I'm just trying to be an important part of his life."

"Important? You're the person he adores more than anyone, more than his own parents, for heaven's sake. You really need to back off!"

"Never," replied Paul angrily. "I owe him all the attention I can give him."

"Owe him? What are you talking about? You've given him more than any grandparent could. Sometimes I wonder about you." Julie took a deep breath and continued, "Okay, go on your trip, but I think you should step back a little when you return. Even Megan thinks you're too much with Danny."

"Yeah, well, I don't!" shouted Paul, as he left the house to pick up his grandson for the first of his many planned outings with the youngster.

* * *

Every time Paul saw his grandson he marveled at the boy's appearance, because it seemed to change in a variety of ways. His hair was light brown one moment and dark the next. His eyes appeared to vary in color—hazel, then brown, and then blue. What intrigued Paul the most was how his grandson's body alternated from wispy to stocky. *Kids are like chameleons. They change before your eyes*, he thought, as he gazed at Danny, who dashed ahead of him through the Berkshire County entrance to the nation's longest stretch of conservation trail.

"Are we going to hike down to Georgia?" asked Danny, excitedly pointing to a map that displayed the trail's trajectory.

"Wish we could, but that would take us weeks. Maybe when you're a little older," replied Paul, his heart nearly bursting with affection for his cherished grandchild. "But we'll actually be hiking to another state, Connecticut."

"Wow!" responded Danny, delightedly. "You're the best grandpa in the world!"

The child's affectionate words caused tears to well up in Paul's eyes, and when he averted his gaze to conceal his emotion, the old but still horrific image of what might have been reasserted itself as it had hundreds of times before. *God, no! God, no!* Paul thought, his body stiffening.

"And you're the best grandson in the world," he replied, following a pause to regain his composure.

After hiking several miles, Paul and Danny pitched their tent at a trail campground and gulped down sandwiches and brownies packed for the first leg of their journey.

"Grandpa, I wrote you a poem," announced Danny, removing a piece of paper from his backpack.

"Really?" said Paul, overjoyed. "Well, please read it to me."

"Okay," said Danny, taking a deep breath. *"My grandpa is like no other in the whole wide world. He gives me everything there is and much more, like a new bike, soccer stuff, and other great things. He is the most fun to be with. Better than anyone there is."*

His grandson's paean left him speechless and he wrapped his arms around him and held him tightly. Shortly after the moon appeared, Paul and Danny slipped into their sleeping bags and quickly fell asleep, exhausted from their long day's blissful explorations.

In the morning, as they crawled from their sleeping bags, Paul noticed that

Danny's hair had turned a bright golden yellow.

"Kids are amazing the way they keep changing," he commented, as his grandson took a large bite from an apple. "You're God's most amazing creatures."

"Come on, grandpa. We got to get going," said Danny, standing.

"Really, really amazing. Like a mirage or something," mumbled Paul, seeing that his grandson was considerably taller than he had been the previous day.

* * *

It was mid-morning when Paul realized that his grandson had disappeared from the trail behind him. He called his name but there was no reply, so he began to retrace his steps. Occasionally he encountered other hikers and asked if they had seen his grandson but none had.

"I saw you at camp this morning, but I don't recall seeing a kid with you," reported one hiker.

"He would be kind of hard to remember, because he never looked the same," replied Paul, inspiring a curious look from the man.

Panic began to take hold of Paul as he went further back on the trail without finding any evidence of his grandson. Finally he reached the spot where he and Danny had spent the night, but the site was empty. He had hoped to recruit the aid of the park ranger he had seen the day before yet he, too, was nowhere to be found.

"Danny! Danny!" he kept shouting at the top of his lungs, but the forest remained eerily quiet.

Paul stood alone in the deserted encampment for several minutes scanning the landscape in every direction.

"Where are you, Danny? Don't do this to your grandpa. Come back . . .

come back. I'll be better. Give me another chance," he pleaded, eventually giving in to an overwhelming urge to lie in the grass and shut his eyes. "Why did you leave your grandpa?" he whimpered, as exhaustion brought him sleep.

He was awakened by a voice calling his name.

"Danny? Is it you, Danny?" he replied, shaking the cobwebs from his brain.

"Stop it! Stop it right now, Paul!" snapped his wife.

"Have they found him?" inquired her husband, desperately.

"Found him? What are you talking about? You're in one of your stupors again," snarled Julie, who was seated across from him.

A glass window separated the couple, and a large uniformed man stood to Paul's rear.

"He's lost. Our little Danny is gone?" said Paul urgently, his agitation rapidly mounting.

Julie exhaled deeply and moved her head closer to the window.

"Yes, he is lost . . . *forever*," she responded, tears forming in her eyes.

"What do you mean?"

"You threw him to the floor and killed him. He was just a little baby," said Julie, now sobbing. "You know that. For God's sake, you know that."

"No!" screamed Paul, leaping to his feet and pounding at the window. "I love Danny. I would never hurt him!"

Shedding Light

The cemetary is an open space among the ruins . . .
—Percy Bysshe Shelley

Margaret Hamlin lived across the street from a small, centuries-old cemetery. Its neglected appearance had disturbed her since she'd moved into her house. In the beginning she tried to avoid looking at the burial ground but found it impossible, since her large bay window faced it. Keeping the drapes closed only made the living room in her house dreary during the day, and she found the idea of having to turn on the lights before nightfall depressing.

Eventually she decided on a solution to the problem—she would spruce up the graveyard. She began to pull the weeds surrounding the headstones, planting colorful flowers in a few strategic spots.

Despite her efforts, the cemetery remained a gloomy and forlorn patch of land for half the year, given the frigid northern Wisconsin winters. The cold gave it a bareness that accentuated the leaning and decrepit monuments and made Margaret all the more mindful of the ancient remains beneath them. In the twilight shadows, the headstones took on an even more disturbing aspect. To her, the dead appeared unearthed . . . as if risen out of some kind of profound sadness.

It was then that Margaret decided to take further action. She would add lights, colored lights, in an attempt to change the bleak aura that hung over the resting place of people that once had likely lived on the very land her house now sat on.

Why do graveyards have to be such lonely, foreboding places? she wondered, on her way to the local hardware store. *Didn't the deceased once revel in the joys of life? Why are they depicted in such melancholy and grim terms? We die, but does it change who we were? We no longer breathe but does that turn us into something terrible . . . monsters?*

"I hate those horror movies. Zombies . . . my word," she grumbled, as she pulled into Ryerson's Variety Emporium, determined more than ever to give the old graveyard a facelift.

In short order, Margaret found strings of tinted bulbs and spotlights, *but how would she light them so far away?* she pondered.

"Could probably use a heavy duty extension cord," said the young clerk. "We got a hundred-footer. You could connect a couple of them if you need real length. Cars will just roll over them. Shouldn't cause a disconnection. What are you using them for?"

"Oh, just want to decorate something across from my house," answered Margaret, evasively.

"Well, all these pretty lights should do the trick."

"I hope so," said Margaret, paying for her goods. "If not, I'll be back for more."

* * *

The next morning Margaret unraveled the long extension cords, and, to her great satisfaction, found that they reached the cemetery with room to spare. She then draped the colored lights over several tombstones, arranging two spotlights to splash a glow over the lot.

When evening arrived, she excitedly hit the switch. To her delight, what had been a dreary chasm was transformed into a luminous tableau.

"Oh my, how wonderful! That's how it should be. Not a place of gloom and doom, for heaven's sake."

The few cars that typically used the road slowed as they passed the illuminated resting place. Each subsequent evening, more cars appeared, some pulling to a stop to take in the full effect. One driver parked his car and followed the extension cord to Margaret's house to express his satisfaction with her handiwork.

"Never did see a cemetery all lit up like that. It sure does make you feel better about those sad places," he said with a broad smile that brought one to Margaret's face.

That night, Margaret decided to add more lights to brighten some of the monuments at the far reaches of the graveyard. *No reason anyone should be neglected,* she thought, feeling happier than she had in a long time. Life had mostly been a burden to Margaret since her retirement and divorce. It had been ages since she experienced a sense of purpose, and illuminating the graveyard gave her one.

* * *

News of her deed spread, and she found herself the subject of an interview in the local newspaper. The reporter, Deek Bellows, asked what motivated Margaret to decorate the cemetery and she enthusiastically gave a full account.

"Well, it does make sense that the living should make an effort to improve the resting places of the departed. They sure can be pretty dreary," observed

Bellows, who then posed another question. "Do you know there's a pretty notorious character buried there?"

"No, I didn't. Who might that be?"

"Seymour Cowley. Killed his wife and daughter and then took his own life. They're buried there with him up in back, I think. Apparently he acted out of fear that his family had smallpox. Really was chicken pox though. A terrible tragedy. Names are pretty much worn off their headstones, but some old folk around here still know the story of Crazy Cowley, as he came to be called. Come to think of it, they may not take too kindly to your prettying up the place or drawing attention to it. Was a pretty big shock and embarrassment to the town when it happened all those years ago. You can imagine."

"I had no idea," responded Margaret, taken aback by the information.

The reporter left her feeling somewhat conflicted about her work on the graveyard, but eventually she came to the conclusion that it didn't matter that one of its occupants had committed murder. What was important to Margaret was that he had done so thinking he was sparing his family the pain of a horrible disease. In her mind the act had even been heroic. It soon became apparent to Margaret that others didn't feel that way. Shortly after she'd had her lunch, the doorbell rang.

"Hello, Mrs. Hamlin. I'm here to ask you to remove those lights from the cemetery," said a middle-aged man in coveralls.

"Well, why should I do that?" inquired Margaret, blocking the entrance to her house.

"'Cause it ain't right. That's why."

"What isn't right?"

"To be making something of that wicked place," grumbled the man.

"Wicked? What's so wicked about a little graveyard?"

"Crazy Cowley's buried there, and he murdered his kin."

"And how do you know that?" asked Margaret, beginning to feel her blood rise.

"He was my great uncle twice removed. Gave my ancestors nothing but heartbreak with what he done. My mama heard about you prettying up his grave and she near fainted. Had me come over here to get you to stop."

"Look, Mr. . . . ?"

"Crowley. Just like . . . like *him*" said the man, pointing in the direction of the cemetery. "I'm Edward though."

"Mr. Crowley . . . *Edward*," Margaret proceeded, "there are other people buried there, too. Besides, what your relative did wasn't without compassion. He thought his family was dying from smallpox and didn't want them to suffer. It was a terrible misunderstanding."

"Maybe so, but he killed them just the same and gave the Crowley name a bad reputation. We don't need to remind people of that by your making a carnival of the place."

"I'm doing no such thing. I'm just trying to make it . . . well, less gloomy," defended Margaret.

"That's what it's supposed to be. Dead people are there. It's not an amusement park, for mercy's sake. Just get them blasted lights out of there. Besides, ain't your kin buried there. You only been here for a while and want to change things that ain't your business."

The man turned and quickly strode to his parked pickup truck. Margaret was tempted to call after him that she had no intention of removing the lights but she kept quiet. When he sped away she gave her door a good hard slam.

"The audacity," she mumbled, pouring herself a rare third cup of coffee.

* * *

For the balance of the day she fumed over the encounter, and when nightfall came, it gratified her to turn on the cemetery lights. *Revenge is sweet*, she told herself.

"There you go, folks. Enjoy the deserved attention," said Margaret, with uncharacteristic bravado.

She turned off the living room lamp and dragged a chair over to the bay window. There she sat observing the cars as they meandered by the cemetery. By the time she was ready to go to bed, she calculated the number of cars passing her house had doubled since the first day she brightened up the burial ground. It filled her with pride that her effort was causing people to have more appreciation of the resting place of the long departed.

Poor forgotten souls . . . no one should ever be ignored because they're gone, thought Margaret, finally going to bed and quickly slipping into a deep, satisfying sleep. It was past eight when she woke up and the sunlight in the room caused her to squint as she reached for her robe.

The cemetery lights, she recalled, *I need to turn them off.* As she looked out of her second floor bedroom window, Margaret noticed an object on her lawn but could not make it out. *I need new glasses. Better make an appointment with the eye doctor.* From her living room she was able to identify what was in front of her house. *What the . . . ?* The strings of colored lights, spotlights, and extension cords were neatly stacked next to the birdbath. It immediately occurred to Margaret that Edward Crowley had taken action into his own hands. *Well, that's not going to happen, fella.* After she downed a cup of coffee, she returned the lights to their original location, vowing to stay awake that night to confront Crowley, if he returned.

* * *

As soon as the late day sun fell behind the pine trees, Margaret hit the switch to light the graveyard. She sat at the bay window and poured herself a hot cup of cocoa from the thermos she had filled in anticipation of a long night. Cars soon began to appear on the street. At one point, she counted seven vehicles parked in front of the cemetery and again she felt great satisfaction. It was well after midnight when the last car left the site and despite filling herself with caffeine, Margaret had to fight to remain awake and ultimately lost the battle. She awoke as dawn was breaking.

"Shoot!" she blurted, again finding the cemetery lighting coiled up on her lawn.

She dressed quickly and reconnected the lights to the graveyard. She then located Edward Crowley's address in the phone book and drove to his house. A woman Margaret assumed was his wife answered the door and without hesitation invited her inside. Mrs. Crowley called for her husband, who immediately emerged from the kitchen.

"Can I help you, Mrs. Hamlin?" asked Crowley, with a sour look.

"Yes, indeed, you can, Mr. Crowley. I would greatly appreciate it if you would stop removing the lights from the cemetery. You know why I put them there, and although you have your reasons for not liking them, everyone else in town seems to appreciate them."

"I don't know what you're talking about. I haven't done nothing like that," protested Crowley, with a sincerity that surprised her and made her doubt her conviction.

"Well, if you didn't, who did?"

"Maybe someone else don't like all the attention you're bringing to that old bone yard. But I can tell you it ain't me pulling them lights off. I got better things to do with my time, like getting to work right now," said Crowley, turning his back to Margaret and disappearing from the room.

"Is there anything else I can do for you?" asked Mrs. Crowley, sweetly.

"No, sorry to bother you," replied Margaret, feeling awkward.

If he didn't do it, who did? wondered Margaret on her drive home. *Probably some kids pulling a prank.*

* * *

That evening the largest crowd ever gathered at the graveyard. The visitors were mostly teenagers and left their cars to romp through the headstones with music blaring from a boom box. The partying went on until late at night, and Margaret was tempted to confront the revelers but resisted the urge to do so fearing the consequences.

"So disrespectful," Margaret mumbled, finally climbing into bed after things had quieted down.

Not long after she had drifted off, a loud crash caused her to sit bolt upright. Glass from the shattered window covered her bedspread. At the foot of the bed was one of the graveyard spotlights. Margaret pushed the covers aside and walked carefully to the broken window. What she saw outside caused her to gasp. *It can't be! Impossible!* Standing under her bedroom window was a decomposed figure in a rotted waistcoat.

"LET US REST IN PEACE!" bellowed the reanimated corpse, which turned and lurched back toward the cemetery.

"Crazy Crowley, is that you?" shouted Margaret, causing the cadaver to stop and glance back at her malevolently.

It then vanished into the darkness.

"Well, be that way," grumbled Margaret, indignantly.

As expected she found the cemetery lights on her lawn when morning arrived. Instead of restoring them yet again, she put them in the garage.

"You try to do something nice, and this is what you get . . ." she huffed. Margaret returned to her house and closed the curtains in her living room.

They stayed that way for some years until it came her time to occupy a forgotten plot of earth.

The Nature of Things

*The bird forlorn
That singeth with her breast against a thorn*
—Thomas Hood

The unobstructed horizon of western Nebraska inspired Emil Blanding like nothing he had ever experienced. He had spent his whole life in the forested hills of Upstate New York and had always felt constricted, if not suffocated, by the crowded landscape. From the time he was a young child he had longed for the open spaces of the kind he saw in his geography books and in western movies and TV shows.

When his family drove cross-country to visit an uncle in Cheyenne, Wyoming, Emil fell in love with the high plains that spread majestically from the central region of the Cornhusker state to the eastern foothills of the Rocky Mountains. His parents and sister were at a loss to understand Emil's appreciation for the parched and empty grasslands.

"I think it's ugly. There's no trees or anything. Just some cows," observed his younger sibling, scrunching her brow disapprovingly.

"They're not cows. They're cattle grazing on the open range," replied Emil, defensively.

"Where'd you get that from, son?" asked Mr. Blanding.

"What?"

"*Cattle grazing on the open range.* Sounds like something out of a Zane Grey novel. You ever read any of his stuff?"

"No. I saw it in my geography book," replied Emil, drinking in the passing countryside.

"I think cattle are the only thing that would want to live out here," said Mrs. Blanding.

"I want to live here, and someday I will," declared Emil.

"Well, I won't visit you if you do," chided nine-year-old Carrie.

"Good," blurted Emil. "That's why I'm moving here."

"I don't know why you're so attracted to this place," remarked Emil's mother.

"There's just something here. I don't know."

"Hey, sport, you should live wherever you want, but at twelve years old you have plenty of time to figure that out."

But Emil *had* figured it out and remained committed to the idea throughout junior high and vocational-technical school where he majored in highway construction. Within a month of graduation, he had located a job with the Nebraska Department of Roads to assist the survey crew in the construction of a single lane blacktop located twenty miles east of the Wyoming border near the tiny town of Elton. It was exactly the part of the country that had held so much allure for him. And to make things even better, the two-room furnished apartment that had been arranged for him featured a view of the region's endless vistas.

"Beautiful," muttered Emil, as he drank in the infinite plains beyond his window. "Just beautiful."

* * *

Having arrived in Elton on a Saturday, Emil had the rest of the weekend to explore the area before reporting to work at the construction site. He had dreamed of owning a small ranch with horses, and the next day as the sun rose, he set out to find the perfect location. Emil calculated that it would take a year before he could put a down payment on a piece of land. After that he planned to save up to build a house and stable. He had driven north about ten miles when he spotted a *For Sale* sign along a small rise in the road.

Ten acres here would be perfect, thought Emil, examining the rolling bluff. By the look of the faded letters on the sign, the land had been available for a while, and he hoped it would still be unclaimed when he was in a position to buy it. By the end of the day, Emil had come across several more appealing pieces of land for sale, and he felt exhilarated by the prospect of someday owning one of them. As the sun set over the far horizon, Emil sat in the window of his apartment and imagined riding his horse in the vast open spaces. When he turned in for the night, his dreams continued the fantasy.

* * *

Emil arrived at the work site an hour before anyone else. The second person to appear was Sam Falker, the crew chief, with whom Emil had spoken on the phone.

"Emil, right? He asked, extending his hand in greeting. "Well, you're an eager beaver. Hope it rubs off on the other guys. Pretty sluggish bunch first thing in the morning, 'specially on Mondays. So you found Elton okay?"

"Yes sir," answered Emil, who was cut off before he could say anything further.

"And the apartment suits you? No rats or bed bugs?" laughed Falker.

"No sir . . ."

"Celia don't allow no vermin in her place. That's a guarantee. Never met a woman so hell bent on killing the world's bacteria."

"It's very . . ."

"She can tell you all about the town, not that there's much to tell. Lived here her full seventy years."

As Falker continued, two dusty pickups pulled up.

"There's some of the laggards now. Hey Ben and Jeff come meet the greenhorn."

After an exchange of greetings, Falker assigned Emil to Ben, telling them to work the far south end of the planned road.

"Get me some positions out there and measure the rise in Buck Creek."

The terrain leading to the location was relatively smooth with the exception of occasional ruts that caused the front end of Ben's well-worn Ford F150 to slam with a force that threatened to shatter the tailbones of its occupants.

"She's got 243,000 miles on her, so she ain't got a lot bounce left," remarked Ben, with a chuckle at Emil's obvious discomfort. "So why'd the heck you want to move to this dusty part of the country?"

"Well, the job. Not easy to find one back in New York State. And I like the wide-open spaces. When I was through here with my family years ago, it really appealed to me. Too many trees back east."

"Hell, we could use a few here. Trying to find some shade in the heat ain't easy. Just look out there. Only shade is along the creek, and then it ain't a whole lot of help dodging the sun."

* * *

It took the better part of an hour to reach their destination, and by then Emil was eager to dispel the numbness that had accrued in his lower back.

"Let's mark some points from that rock down about 200 yards to the bend," instructed Ben, collecting equipment from the bed of his pickup.

Emil walked ahead to the first survey point and spotted what looked like a bird's nest at the base of the rock. When he got closer, he noticed movement, and then an object fluttered by his head, causing him to crouch. Coming up behind him, Ben went to the nest and picked it up. It contained two small brown eggs.

"Kirtland warblers. You didn't see this, okay?" said Ben, chucking the nest into the creek.

"Why'd you do that?" responded Emil, surprised.

"They're a project killer. The tree huggers will block construction if they know about this. We're out of a job then. So this didn't happen . . . *understand*?"

"Why?"

"They're a so-called *endangered* species and their habitat can't be disturbed. We'd have to redirect construction to the other side of the creek and that would cost tons of dough and end the project," explained Ben, searching around the rock for other signs of the rare bird.

Not far away, Emil discovered another nest but said nothing to Ben. He could not abide another one being destroyed. At midday, Sam Falker showed up and inquired about their progress.

"We found a warbler's nest and got rid of it. I told the kid to say nothing about it," reported Ben.

"Yeah, keep quiet about that or we're all on unemployment. If the Nebraska Wildlife Federation gets ahold of this we're done for. No problem, *right*, Emil?"

"Sure," replied Emil, feeling conflicted.

"Good. Now let's have some lunch, and then I'll check out what you done.

Hope you got the measurements nailed this time. Your tuning was way off on Friday, Ben."

"The leveling instrument was damaged, Sam. I told you that," protested Ben.

"Nothing about you is on the level, Ben," teased Sam.

"You're a little over-triangulated yourself, boss," replied Ben, digging into his lunch box.

The levity continued between the two men but did nothing to dispel Emil's growing concern over what was being done to the imperiled fowl along the intended path of the blacktop. By week's end, he had discovered two more warbler nests and had placed them out of harm's way. Meanwhile, Ben had come upon another with chicks and took great pleasure in stomping them to oblivion. When Emil expressed his disgust with Ben's violent action, the older man accused him of being a "green fiend."

"What?" replied Emil, still angered by the horrible spectacle he had just witnessed.

"You know, one of them nature freaks who cries if you step on an ant."

"I just don't like to see innocent animals slaughtered."

"Innocent, my ass! Them birds will take the money out of your pockets if the wrong people find out they're here. And don't you go saying *nothing* about it, either. Shoot, Emil stop being such a little piss pants. You want this job, don't you?" asked Ben, challengingly.

"I like the job, I just don't . . ."

"Well, then stop making an issue out of a few friggin' birds. Keep your eye on the big picture. It's called a paycheck."

* * *

Emil's landlady, Celia Bell, reminded him of his grandmother with her white hair pulled back in a bun. When he returned after a day's work, she greeted him warmly from her front porch rocker. After the first couple of greetings, Emil sat on the steps and engaged her in conversation about Elton and the countryside around it.

"You sure do seem interested in this old town, and that's really kind of you. Most of the tenants I've had didn't care a peep about Elton."

"I love the high plains and want to build a house out there in all that space," said Emil, pointing in the direction of the empty horizon.

"Well, that's sure something. Most young fellows want to be in the big city."

Celia had asked Emil to join her for supper after his first day on the job, but he had declined out of bashfulness. Eventually, she wore him down, and he ate with her almost nightly. It was on such an occasion that he asked her about the Kirtland warblers.

"Those little devils almost cost us a living. The NWF made a big stink about building the road to Hornbill, and almost got it shut down. They come around sometimes to check for nests. But we make sure they don't find none. Bunch of town folks go out hunting for the pests and clear them out so them people can't raise a ruckus."

It depressed Emil to find Celia so insensitive to the plight of the threatened birds. His opinion of her quickly changed, and he stopped taking meals with her.

"You got to eat, son. Why don't you want to have dinner?" she inquired.

"I eat a lot for lunch, because I get really hungry by then. So I'm trying not to eat anything at night to keep from gaining more weight. I've been losing the battle of the bulge my whole life, and eating before turning in puts the pounds on you real fast," offered Emil.

Celia accepted his excuse reluctantly and thereafter he noticed a lack of warmth in her nightly greeting. Emil would sneak some items from the local convenience store for his evening meal. He avoided cooking anything, fearing Celia would pick up the scent and realize he was eating after all.

* * *

A month into his job, Emil calculated that he had saved two-dozen warblers from the heel of his fellow worker. Despite this, Ben still had managed to eliminate several nests and their contents. It was obvious to Emil that his cohort took great pleasure in annihilating the helpless creatures, and it was all he could do to contain his anger toward him.

In phone calls to his parents, Emil said nothing of the situation, omitting the fact that he was on the verge of throwing in the towel and returning home. Watching Ben's atrocities had taken the joy out of living in the place he loved. Every act of cruelty toward the helpless birds left a stain on his beloved plains, nearly ruining them for him.

On the morning of the day Emil planned to quit his job, he was awakened by a tapping sound against his bedroom window. A yellow-breasted Kirtland warbler was on the windowsill. Emil rose from bed and moved slowly to the window as the small bird continued to peck at the glass. He was surprised and pleased that it remained in place even when just the windowpane separated them. It was only when Emil opened the window that the warbler disappeared. When he shut the window, it returned. Again he gently raised the window a crack, and this time the bird flew into his room, landing on the bed. As Emil approached it, it flew back to the windowsill. In the seconds that followed, the two stared at one another, and Emil felt a profound connection with the animal.

The surreal moment was suddenly broken when the bristles of a broom struck the window, pressing down on the warbler.

"Got you!" shouted Celia.

In horror, Emil ran to the window and opened it wider. The warbler fell inside to the floor.

"I'm coming in. Just made five dollars," said Celia gleefully.

Emil picked up the lifeless warbler and put it in his pocket as Celia entered.

"Where is he?" she asked, her eyes searching the floor.

"It flew out," replied Emil, sensing the bird in his pocket.

"Damn!" mumbled Celia, deeply disappointment. "If you hadn't opened that window I'd have gotten him and been richer for it."

"Five dollars? Who gives you that?" inquired Emil.

"Sam Falker," answered Celia matter-of-factly, looking out the window to the ground below it. "Shoot, I had the little bugger, too."

When the elderly woman left Emil's room, he carefully removed the warbler from his pocket placing it on the windowsill. The moment he did, it sprung to life, but rather than quickly fly away, it looked up at Emil.

"Go," urged Emil fearing Celia would return.

The warbler did as it was asked.

* * *

On his way to the construction site to tender his resignation, Emil saw that the bird was flying alongside his car.

"Hey there, little friend," Emil mumbled. "Don't think you better go where I'm going. Not safe for you."

As Emil drew within a couple miles of his destination, he was startled to see that dozens of other warblers were now following him. By the time he reached the construction site, the sky was swarming with birds swooping up and down in perfect formation. Their extraordinary mass darkened the ground as they dove toward the office trailer.

What the hell is happening? wondered Emil, climbing from his vehicle.

Ben and Sam were standing next to their pickup trucks when the birds mounted a blitzkrieg, showering them with poo.

"*What the . . .!*" screamed Ben, attempting to cover himself while Sam reached desperately for the door of his truck.

Before they could reach shelter the feathered armada unleashed another round of feces at them. Both men fell to the ground drenched in bird excrement and whining like babies. Although Emil had been standing only feet from them, he had not been touched by the bombardment. After a third assault, the birds flew away having clearly achieved their mission.

"Give us a hand over here!" shouted Sam, attempting to regain his footing in the slippery droppings that covered the ground.

"I quit," replied Emil, returning to his car.

As he drove from the site, a vehicle approached his. On its door were the letters NWF. Emil stopped, rolled down the window, and shouted to the driver.

"There's an endangered species back there covered in warbler poop!"

On his return to Elton, Emil was rejoined by what he was certain was the Kirtland warbler that had appeared on his windowsill. When he slowed to make the turn that led back to town, the bird landed on his hood. It then flew off in the opposite direction.

"Okay," said Emil. "I'm going where you're going."

And they both—*man and animal*—moved toward a higher plain.

What He Remembered...

Lace curtains swaying in the breeze
the maple armoire caressed.
Sun bleeding through the stained glass
her fragrance on the bed sheets.
Wilting roses in an orange Savoy vase
narrow fingers wiping his brow.
Mozart concertos coaxing his heartbeats
breathing chastened by infirmity.
Whispering voices in dark corners
tired eyes on vital signs.
Fear rising and ebbing in tidal waves
furious dreams awake and sleeping.
Grandson's kiss on a hirsute earlobe
vendors along a Moroccan street.
Raven at the windowsill set for flight
fading hosannas and valedictions.

Michael C. Keith is the author of over 20 books on electronic media, among them *Talking Radio, Voices in the Purple Haze, Radio Cultures, Sounds in the Dark,* and the classic textbook *The Radio Station*. In addition, he coauthored *Waves of Rancor, The Quieted Voice, The Broadcast Century, Global Broadcasting Systems,* and *Dirty Discourse* with Robert Hilliard, *Queer Airwaves* with Phylis Johnson, *Sounds of Change* with Christopher Sterling, and *Norman Corwin's 'One World Flight'* with Mary Ann Watson. The recipient of numerous awards, Keith is also the author of dozens of journal articles and short stories and has served in a variety of editorial positions. In addition, he is the author of a critically acclaimed memoir—*The Next Better Place*, a young adult novel––*Life is Falling Sideways,* and two previous story anthologies—*And Through the Trembling Air* and *Hoag's Object*. He has been nominated for a Pushcart Prize and PEN/O.Henry Award.

The author may be reached via his website:
www.michaelckeith.com